SPINE-CHILLERS

SURREY

Edited by Jenni Bannister

First published in Great Britain in 2016 by:

Remus House
Coltsfoot Drive
Peterborough
PE2 9BF
Telephone: 01733 890066
Website: www.youngwriters.co.uk

Book Design by Ashley Janson

SB ISBN 978-1-78624-121-4

Printed and bound in the UK by BookPrintingUK
Website: www.bookprintinguk.com

Enter, Reader, if you dare...

For as long as there have been stories there have been ghost stories. Writers have been trying scare their readers for centuries using just the power of their imagination. For Young Writers' latest competition Spine-Chillers we asked students to come up with their own spooky tales, but with the tricky twist of using just 100 words!

They rose to the challenge magnificently and this resulting collection of haunting tales will certainly give you the creeps! From friendly ghosts and Halloween adventures to the gruesome and macabre, the young writers in this anthology showcase their creative writing talents.

Here at Young Writers our aim is to encourage creativity and to inspire a love of the written word, so it's great to get such an amazing response, with some absolutely fantastic stories. We will now choose the top 5 authors across the competition, who will each win a Kindle Fire.

I'd like to congratulate all the young authors in *Spine-Chillers - Surrey* - I hope this inspires them to continue with their creative writing. And who knows, maybe we'll be seeing their names alongside Stephen King on the best seller lists in the future...

Jenni Bannister

Editorial Manager

CONTENTS

REIGATE COLLEGE, REIGATE

REIGATE SCHOOL, REIGATE

RICHARD CHALLONER SCHOOL, NEW MALDEN

RYDENS ENTERPRISE SCHOOL & SIXTH FORM COLLEGE, WALTON-ON-THAMES

WOKING COLLEGE, WOKING

THE MINI SAGAS

Out Of The Shadows

The wind howled as she stepped cautiously into the ruined graveyard. 'Hello?' Her voice was wobbly as she called into the black night. No one answered. As she wandered unwillingly past the graves she heard hissing laughter behind her. She whipped around suspiciously. Nothing. The old, beaten church creaked in the background. She stopped at one of the graves. The weather-battered headstone read... her own name! 'Hello? Hello?' she rasped. Suddenly a gloved hand clamped over her mouth and she was dragged into the church. When she was released, she crumpled to the floor and everything went black.

Olivia Owen (12)

A Friend In Need Is A Friend Indeed

I always go to visit her. She brings me great happiness. Every meal time, at 9am, 1pm and at 7pm. I always go to visit her at those times. She's quite quiet, doesn't really say much. I don't think she's feeling well; looking a bit under the weather. She's looking a bit thinner than usual. I wouldn't blame her, I'm sucking up more blood than usual.

Toby Hunt (11)
City of London Freemen's School, Ashtead Park

Little Me

The sun shone on the playground. I skipped to the swings, however a little girl sat there so I headed to the slide but the same girl was ahead of me, menacingly clutching onto her doll. She whispered, 'See you later!' I didn't understand.
That night in bed my eyes closed. I saw the little girl with her doll. At that point I heard the window rattle. Next, I saw the little girl's doll which strangely looked like me. I thought I was hallucinating. *Bang!* The little girl appeared on my bed. 'Goodbye.'

Farrah Preuveneers (11)
City of London Freemen's School, Ashtead Park

Wide Awake

'Come on, Thomas, go to sleep,' I whispered, as I comforted him in his cot. It had been almost an hour now and he still wasn't sleeping. I flicked on the baby monitor and walked downstairs. There was a cry coming from the speaker connected to the baby monitor. I sighed and trudged back up the stairs. Tom's eyes were wide. 'Everything is OK,' I insisted. He wouldn't believe me. Probably because he saw the monster that followed me in.

Samuel Shorrocks (11)
City of London Freemen's School, Ashtead Park

Father's Desperation

My dad had kidney failure, he was desperate for a kidney donor. Desperate. He loved the cellar but weirdly he locked the door. I didn't think much of it until one foggy evening when my dad was showering. I heard peculiar noises coming from the cellar, strangled shrieks and muffled cries. I went to look. Strangely enough the door was unlocked. I shut the door quietly and crept down the stairs. I saw it squirming on the table, its mouth taped shut. There was a jar and in it was Father's desperation. Then I heard all too familiar footsteps.

Abigail Bower (12)
City of London Freemen's School, Ashtead Park

Tick, Tock

Tick tock, tick tock, tick... It stopped. The key wasn't in its usual place. I started to look for it. Suddenly the lights went out. I was home alone without my parents. My heart pounded with fear. After about a minute the lights flickered on. I felt safe again. My parents were meant to be back by now. I wondered where they were.
The next morning I found the key to the clock. Then I opened it. I finally realised why my parents hadn't returned the night before...

Guy Ashworth (12)
City of London Freemen's School, Ashtead Park

Ho, Ho, Ho

The familiar ring of Christmas carols sounded in my ears like a drill. Then an announcement: 'Another child missing, be aware of your children this holiday season.' I didn't let all the fuss interrupt my day and continued as normal. Being Harrods' Santa is so boring when all that children can wish for is safety. Finally the day was over and I arrived home to see policemen at my door. 'Sir, may we search your house?'
'Sure, come in.' They searched every nook and cranny inside my precious home and left. It's fortunate they didn't search the chimney. Merry Christmas.

Jodie Bastow (13)
City of London Freemen's School, Ashtead Park

Dark Night Sky

I was driving home, alone. I turned onto a quiet lane and spotted something on the road. Curious to know more I pulled over and got out. The wind blew and a cold chill ran down my spine. I walked closer to the object. It was a pram. The wind raged again and the pram's wheels turned to reveal a doll. The doll was staring up at the dark sky, its face smashed. I pushed the pram to the side and hurried back to the car. As I pulled off, a small hand gently tapped me on the shoulder.

Aurelia Loth (12)
City of London Freemen's School, Ashtead Park

BREAK OUT

'They're escaping,' Jake screamed. 'Call a chopper, we need to find them!' The prison guards smashed the alarm, hoping the crazed psychopaths would falter in their run through the thick forest surrounding Budapest. The men knew that the prisoners would run a marathon to kill a guard so they were being cautious. They saw a small flash of light from a knife and slowly, stealthily, Jake snuck up to the awaiting prisoner who swung with the speed of a cheetah, trying to kill. The squad opened fire, only to realise the killers had disappeared.

JAMES BARROWS (11)
City of London Freemen's School, Ashtead Park

WELCOME

On my journey from school, I was walking down creepy Milestone Road; haunted, according to locals. *Bang!* Suddenly a ghost appeared before my eyes. 'Welcome.' I jumped back, petrified. *Ridiculous*, I thought, *just the effects of that strange bang. What was that anyway?* I passed through the door to my house and heard the local news on the TV. A boy had been shot. The news replayed the sound of the gunshot at the scene of the murder. *Bang!* Only after hearing that did I remember what the ghost said and how the gunshot sounded awfully familiar. Too familiar.

OLLY LINDQUIST (12)
City of London Freemen's School, Ashtead Park

Slipped

Just like any other school day, I was late, so I put on my orange hoodie and raced down the stairs. Then I slipped. Soon I was limping around the house seeking comfort. I thought I saw my old cat, Patch, but he had died years ago. Suddenly, I heard a scream that was not mine and ran into the hall. My mum and sister were crying. I shouted at them but they did not react. Then I saw what they were looking at. They were staring at a lifeless, body lying limp sprawled across the floor... wearing orange.

Dominic Bunyard (12)
City of London Freemen's School, Ashtead Park

No One Will Know

The mysterious graveyard was a sinister short-cut home for many. A watery, full moon loomed eerily through the murky, dark fog. A sudden blood-curdling howl sliced through the silence and the icy ground shuddered beneath my feet. With a grating creak, the tomb next to me vibrated... shifted... opened! Gravestones collapsed like dominoes. Then out of the tomb rose a little girl, wearing a scarlet robe. Translucent, ghostly, grey; her eyes were empty sockets. At least forty identical ghost children followed her. In unison, they chanted, 'Ssh, ssh, no one will know.' Thunder crashed, then darkness. All were gone!

Oliver Way (12)
City of London Freemen's School, Ashtead Park

The Call

Dripping with blood, he sprinted upstairs. 'Good day?' she called.
'Alright,' he called back, 'I suppose.'
'Dinner's in a few minutes!'
Examining his wound, he turned on the TV, hoping to forget. His mother received a call from his phone. 'Why are you calling? You're only upstairs.'
'Watch out...' was the unfamiliar, chilling reply. Bloodied footprints led her to his room. She opened it in a panic; nothing there. No boy. No dirt. Just a clean, tidy room. The TV was just static and smothered across it in crimson blood, were the words... *watch out!*

Aristeídes Kanavos (12)
City of London Freemen's School, Ashtead Park

It Was Just A Dream

I woke up, sweat dripping from my brow due to a terrifying nightmare: a man with his bare hands, ripped out my heart. I decided to get a drink. However, as I tried to get up, I realised my whole body was pinned to the bed. My breathing increased rapidly. I was being strangled... by nobody. My mouth was dry, no words escaped my lips. Squeezing my eyes shut, I hoped it would stop. Suddenly, I felt breath against my face. I opened my eyes again. A blood-curdling face grinned at me; a pulsing heart in his hand.

Holly Evans (12)
City of London Freemen's School, Ashtead Park

Dreamer Or Screamer?

I picked up a fairground token as I walked towards my favourite ride, the Screamer. I leapt into a cart and buckled myself in. My cart started and zoomed along the track. I was yelling, screaming, having a great time. Near the end of the ride, after many climbs and descents, my cart started to rattle, loudly. I peered in front and saw no more track. Then I started to fall...

I awoke and sat up. I calmed myself down. It was just a dream. Then, I felt something in my pyjama pocket. It was a fairground token...

Tom Hardiman-Evans (11)
City of London Freemen's School, Ashtead Park

Another Me

I'm walking through the woods on my evening walk and I come across a small, magical pond. I approach it and sit down next to it. A calm evening is upon us so I look into the pond and see the moon's reflection. I then catch sight of my own reflection and stare at it for a while. A slight breeze of wind goes past and creates a ripple effect in my reflection. When the pond is calm again, I see myself and also another me stood behind with a big, chintzy smile on its...my face.

Aaron Teale (14)
City of London Freemen's School, Ashtead Park

Phantasm

Walking along the roadside pavement, he knows nothing of what is to come. Normality blinds him, this is his downfall. As his feet alternate between steps, he becomes increasingly delusional, running from what he cannot see. When the mind is hazed by fear of the incomprehensible, no one is trustworthy, nowhere is safe. It's only a matter of time before this victim has to face it. The creature is ready to devour souls, and will not hold back, I guarantee. He walks onwards, unaware. After all, normality is what hides it, they are what feeds it and you're next...

Alexander Pelling (11)
City of London Freemen's School, Ashtead Park

The Doll

On a lovely warm day a group of teenagers were coming back from a carnival. One of them had collected a doll but she didn't really adore it so she threw it in the bin. When the teenagers climbed up the stairs, they noticed that the door was open. All of them rushed in. The light was on and nothing was in there. The light switched off. No one moved. It switched back on and the doll was looking at them. It said, 'Goodnight,' it breathed. They all collapsed down, dead. A solitary floorboard creaked.

Danny Adams (11)
City of London Freemen's School, Ashtead Park

Stopped

Eliza and her family had just finally moved in. On her bed was an old, ragged doll but Eliza put it on the shelf with the others. When she did so, she noticed one of the dolls had the same dress as her. Eliza woke up at midnight to feel cold breath on her face. She opened her eyes to see the doll, hanging from her dream-catcher, its blood-fire eyes burning into hers. The doll whispered, chanted, shrieked. Then suddenly Eliza was china, sitting on the shelf with the other dolls, staring at her bed. Then everything just stopped.

Lily Pearson (11)
City of London Freemen's School, Ashtead Park

You're Doomed

Listen very carefully. Only you must know this. Only you and I know what really happened. Killing me was a big mistake. Before you did it, I trusted you. Every day, I felt safe with you. How could you do such a thing? I thought you were on my side. Now I know differently. Did you consider the consequences of not committing murder properly. You should always check for signs of life, just in case. Only you may regret that you did not. Understand that I am seeking revenge and check the first letter of each sentence; you're doomed!

Alden Horwitz (13)
City of London Freemen's School, Ashtead Park

Ashes To Ashes

It hurt, the constant agony of this sharp pain inside. I could tell there were only a few more breaths I could take. I was stumbling through the piled twigs and tree stumps. I could hear his breath getting closer, I could see the reflection from his torch on his knife. Suddenly I stopped, unable to move, motionless, watching him approach.
I woke unable to breathe, surrounded by wooden walls, hearing the words, 'Ashes to ashes...'

Laura Bacon (12)
City of London Freemen's School, Ashtead Park

The Reappearance

There it was, towering above me. So sturdy and strong. Its presence was overwhelming. Its bricks were cold to touch. At the top a figure was placed. Delicate, hardly visible under the fog. The wind blew suddenly and the little pink doll came drifting towards me. I caught it, I could see it in my arms. Eyes glaring at me, a creepy over-friendly smile. I hated it, for weeks I tried to throw it away but every time it appeared on the wall staring through the window at me.

Megan Haine (13)
City of London Freemen's School, Ashtead Park

Mother?

Almost midnight. A cold, dark graveyard stretching beyond me. A clock strikes the hour. It sends goosebumps running up my spine. Suddenly, repetitive knocking sounds against my mother's tomb. No one in sight. In utter shock and panic, I throw aside the fresh flowers and bury my hands into the rough soil. Despite my reluctance, I am opening the dreaded tomb. Nothing. Nothing but empty space. A hand reaches out, grasping my quivering shoulder. 'You must leave, at once!'
'Mother?' I whisper. No answer. I turn around only to find a foggy night, empty as my mother's tomb.

Freddy Pittman (12)
City of London Freemen's School, Ashtead Park

The Chef's Secret

My dad is head chef at 'End To End', a top restaurant in Guilford. It has just been awarded a Michelin star and tonight all the workers' families are celebrating together with a meal after closing. Dad is famous for cooking the most delicious dishes using organs such as tongue, heart, brain, liver and kidneys. Other chefs want to know Dad's secret for serving food that no one else can match, but he won't say. Perhaps it's because he works so hard, he even has a second job... as an undertaker, preparing bodies for the grave.

Alexander Clark (11)
City of London Freemen's School, Ashtead Park

My Last Breath

He's here again, he's watching me, counting my breaths. I pretend I'm asleep but my heart is beating louder than his echoing footsteps as he walked up the stairs. My body is colder than the freezer that I heard him step out of. The pounding of my head is more rhythmic than the ear piercing screams of my limp parents as they washed the floor a deep red. And my life is ending faster than the glittering knife he plunges deep into my innocent heart. Now I'm just as lifeless as his pale glass-like eyes, which haunt my soul.

Sholeh Eloise Darakhshan (11)
City of London Freemen's School, Ashtead Park

When He Was Here

I'm walking home from school. It's dark, nobody's out, just me. Once I'm home, I open the door. Suddenly, the door slams shut. I guess it's the wind. I shout to see if my parents are in. They're not! I go up to my room but before I touch the door it creaks open. My head peers through the door. I see a black figure. Where does it come from. Don't worry, I found out. 'Little girl, why are you here?' He doesn't give me a chance to speak. His eyes become fixed on me. He comes.

Annie Chesover (12)
City of London Freemen's School, Ashtead Park

Beth

1am. I had been messaging Beth, this beautiful girl who'd asked for my number on Instagram. I thought I recognised her. We talked about everything. In the middle of a conversation I felt someone was watching me. Turning to the window I saw the silhouette of a girl, her face illuminated by a phone. I was petrified. My phone buzzed. The message read 'It's me'. My eyes darted back to the window. She was gone! I heard a noise behind me. Beth stood there, grinning, a knife in her hand. I remembered where I saw her face... on the news.

Erin Warnock (14)
City of London Freemen's School, Ashtead Park

Chased

The clock struck midnight. As I was walking home, I saw a shadow lurking around behind me, watching my every move. I came to a stop and turned around. No one was there. I carried on walking when my phone buzzed; a message from a blocked number. 'I'm behind you'. I turned around, my heart beating through my chest. I ran as fast as I could but stumbled. I slowed down to a walk as I thought I was safe. There was a gentle tap on my shoulder. 'Caught you!' echoed from behind me.

Jessica Widdowson (13)
City of London Freemen's School, Ashtead Park

The Desk

It was an ordinary day at Eastbrook High. Michelle sauntered into the classroom without a care in the world. Something was up. Her classmates were cowering away from her desk. Michelle reached to open it. A gut-wrenching stench wafted out of the desk. A severed head. That was what was inside her desk! The face was familiar. It was a face that she saw every day. It was her father!

Elizabeth Needham (11)
City of London Freemen's School, Ashtead Park

Unexpected Visitor

I sat up in my bed, terrified of the screaming and screeching coming from downstairs. I immediately felt my heart pounding in my chest! I didn't know what to do. I decided to call my neighbour. As soon as I heard a knock on the door, I knew she was here. I had to go downstairs but I really didn't want to. When I reached the last step, the screeching became louder and louder. I peeked a little bit further. To my horror, I saw blood splattered all over the door and a hand lying in the dark, gloomy corridor.

Samaya Bahsoun (12)
City of London Freemen's School, Ashtead Park

The Message

The screen flashed again. It read, 'Meet me at the dump at ten tonight'. So there I was, waiting. The lights flickered off and I was left all alone in the dark. A ghostly face suddenly appeared in front of me. He said nothing. I was just standing, with my mouth dangling open, too frightened to speak. He snapped his fingers and immediately a huge army of black figures appeared behind him. He whistled a tune and they all started walking in sync towards me. I had no time to run because they had grabbed me. It was too late.

Zoe Kilakos (11)
City of London Freemen's School, Ashtead Park

The Matchstick

The whole town's fate depended on this match. I stopped myself. Suddenly, I lost control of my body. Everything I was telling it to do didn't work. I was being possessed! 'Do it,' whispered a voice. It walked me to the house.

'No!' I shouted to myself. It lifted my arm and threw the match. We watched as the house burnt. The fire spread. Minutes passed. It hadn't moved. Townsmen were fleeing. I regained control and a ghostly figure stood in front of me; eyes red, features identical to mine. It whispered in the same voice, 'Done!'

Ambar Vishnoi (11)
City of London Freemen's School, Ashtead Park

Blackout!

Extremely late, one dark, gloomy night. Black! Suddenly the power went off. I was doing my homework and Mum and Dad were fast asleep in bed. I went down the winding, swirling stairs but, oddly, it felt a lot longer to get down them than usual. Finally, I got to the bottom and walked towards the colossal oak door that hid the fuse box behind it. Abruptly, the door swung open in front of my shocked, pale face! What was that? To my horror, I heard a voice, 'Go away, idiot.' It sounded familiar... the voice of my dead brother!

Matthew McEwen (11)
City of London Freemen's School, Ashtead Park

Double

I bought one pair of shoes today, for my son. My only son. When I went to put a name label in the shoes, there were two pairs of exactly the same shoes. I called up to my son. There were two deafening answers, of the exact same voice. When I looked up the stairs, the lights turned out. Mist filled the dark, gloomy staircase. There were two pairs of laser eyes staring at me. It was my nightmare of murder come true.

Juliette Lawrence (12)
City of London Freemen's School, Ashtead Park

The Last Breath

Bleep, the screen flashed with another notification. I finally found the courage to pick the phone up. Red flashing words, the message: 'Beware, it's your turn soon'. My heart instantly started pounding. *Tap, tap, tap.* In seconds it started screaming louder than ever before. I shuffled over slowly, dodging the creaky floorboards, to where the sound was coming from. *Tap, tap.* This time louder. A woman with frosty coloured skin, knotted black hair and sooty chains wrapped around her body, stood by the smashed window. 'Let me in, honey. I've had my nightmare, now it's your turn.'

Zara Agius (11)
City of London Freemen's School, Ashtead Park

Where Am I?

Walking home on a cool, dark October evening and nobody is outside, only silence. I feel I'm being watched. A cool, eerie mist comes swirling towards me. A shiver goes through me. Suddenly, I hear footsteps behind me. Looking back I see nobody! Speeding up, the footsteps quicken too. The hoot of an owl frightens me. My heart is thumping. Then, ahead I see my father... although he died two years ago. I run towards him. As I approach, he disappears. Shadows follow me. Next I become unconscious. Everything is happening too fast, everyone's crowding around. I can't breathe.

Amélie King (11)
City of London Freemen's School, Ashtead Park

THE VISITOR

The bell unexpectedly rang, the lights flickered, plunging the room into darkness. The windows slammed shut and the door creaked open. The words flashed onto the screen and the entire class screamed. Standing in the doorway was a dark, incomplete shadow. The ghost of James O'Marley had returned. It was exactly twelve years since James was violently shoved over the sports hall balcony. Immediately alarm bells rang inside my head. Every year O'Marley would select one innocent child and feed on the purity of their soul. This year it was me.

HANNAH ARTER (11)
City of London Freemen's School, Ashtead Park

YOU'RE NEXT...

She went her locker to get out her chemistry book, entered the code and pulled open the door. Staring at her was a head, hanging where her backpack normally went. Stuck to it was a post-it with 'You're next!' written on it. She ran to her sister's class; I followed. She quickly turned the handle. The lights were low, a spotlight was on her sister's pale face. 'You're next.' She screamed. The lights turned fully off. All I heard were a few screams then it ended. It all ended.

KIARA VALKENBURG (11)
City of London Freemen's School, Ashtead Park

Little Girl

I heard it: a scream. I crept up to the house. The door creaked open. There I saw her, a white-faced girl, staring at me. 'I'm alone,' she muttered. I took her to the car, still staring at me. The car jolted; it wouldn't start. I felt intimidated. 'Little girl, stop staring,' I said sternly. I tried to get out but the car was locked. I tried again. She tilted her head and smiled. I plunged into darkness. I heard: 'I'm alone.'

Lauren Baker (11)
City of London Freemen's School, Ashtead Park

The Strangeness Of Death

I awoke to hear a scream from my bed. My thoughts clouded, I drifted upwards; finding myself watching my daughter enter my bed. Flying towards the door, I found a blood-drenched dagger pointing towards a picture of me on the wall. I flew back into bed, only for a slowly materialising, white mist to cover me. My daughter's voice echoed. 'Daddy, you look like you're a fancy dress ghost. You're white as a sheet. Why aren't your legs touching the ground?' I felt like I had been spoken to as if I were Death himself. I now was Death himself.

James Percival (11)
City of London Freemen's School, Ashtead Park

THE CRUCIFIX

The priest strolled in, locked the door with a solid clunk behind him. He sat down peacefully for his prayers. As he was ending, a blood-curdling scream ripped apart the calm. The priest turned around. The door was open. He shuddered over to the door and saw blood-stained footsteps heading to the locked chapel. The door opened then closed. The priest hurried to the chapel door and looked in. Blood came from her mouth. Her hands were nailed to the cross. Her body limp, her shadow still stood behind her. Or did it?

PETER COCKS (14)
City of London Freemen's School, Ashtead Park

THE COLD HARD GLOWING STARE

The glowing eyes stared cold and hard at my quaking body, my insides churning. Less than thirty minutes ago I was staring dead hard at the TV, plate before of me, eyes glued to the screen. I heard a knock, a soft knock at the door. Stumbling over, only to find a cold, deserted, empty street, I returned to the film I was indulged in. A woman stood, black haired with cold, white, chilling skin, her red eyes glowed like fire. There was a scream then darkness. All there was to be seen was the glowing irises of the girl.

FREJA FORREST (12)
City of London Freemen's School, Ashtead Park

Alice

'Time of death, 6.06 am.' The doctors have left to inform Alice's parents. I am alone with her. I start to weep; my only friend is dead. I feel her cold hand on mine. Startled I wipe my tears, relief flooding through me. She's alive! Moving slowly, my friend sits up and turns her head towards me. She is staring at me, her eyes as black as night, unnaturally dark. Slowly I see her pull the dagger from her heart and she advances, blade pointing towards me. Then she emits a low, chilling rasp. 'You're next.'

Abby Graham-Maw (12)
City of London Freemen's School, Ashtead Park

Our Dream House

My mum and dad just bought our dream house. It is an old townhouse in Picadilly. It's a beautiful old house; five bedrooms, two baths. We started moving in today. All there is is a TV and an air mattress. We were watching TV in the dark before it was time to sleep. All of a sudden they heard the patter of little feet. The door slammed shut and they heard the bell ring and the laughter of a child. The thing is, they have no children.

Izzy Mitchell (13)
City of London Freemen's School, Ashtead Park

THE RUMOURS

Today was one strange day. It all started when I took my dog for a walk on the common. There were always rumours about the common, rumours saying there were monsters and ghosts there. I'd never believed them till today. I met a girl on the common. She was wearing a torn dress with blood-red stains. I asked her about it and about why she was barefoot. 'Why aren't you?' she asked dully. Suddenly the sky turned grey, smothered with clouds. More people emerged wearing torn clothes, walking slowly, lifelessly. I ran. I lost them. I escaped that horrid nightmare.

AMY KEEN (12)
City of London Freemen's School, Ashtead Park

THE VISITORS

One night there was a boy in his bed. At 9.45 he gota message saying 'Sorry, son' from his parents. He put his phone down and drifted back to sleep.
Later he woke up at 6.30 and his dad stumbled into the room saying, 'I have to go.' He vanished.
Twenty minutes later his mum came in and said, 'At 9.45 I distracted your dad while driving and he hit another car and spun off the motorway. We will never be found so please stay safe. I can finally talk to you because I recently died at 6.30.'

MATTHEW THOMAS (11)
City of London Freemen's School, Ashtead Park

Dead Man Walking

Dead. Dead was my father at the age of just 60. I couldn't believe it, as I laid the flowers on the cold stone. I began to walk home and stumbled up the path to my house. I looked up and there I saw him, standing there, his decaying, yet still recognisable face, staring at me. The face of my dead father looked down on me.

Adam Coates (13)
City of London Freemen's School, Ashtead Park

Locked In...

It was around 1am. I was driving back from a party when I turned down an alleyway shortcut but it was dark and foggy. The ghostly street lights lit up a white figure at the end of the alley. It was a woman who seemed to have lost her way. It was pouring with rain so I asked her where she was headed. 'Mulgrave Road,' she replied. 'Hop in,' I said. I locked all the doors and grinned. 'Never ride with a stranger!' I chuckled. All time became frozen. Blood splattered the windows. 'Time for my next pick up,' I smiled.

Lydia Maria Mustafa (14)
City of London Freemen's School, Ashtead Park

THE SHADOW

I am racing through the moonlit hallway; a shadow is scrambling, clawing its way towards me. I shiver with anxiety - who knows what will happen? I want to tear away from this beast but it is scratching against my heels. I try to fight my way into the nearest ward. As I struggle through the doorway, I gaze upon the limp, lifeless bodies attached to the everlasting drips. It's pinning me down, revealing nothing but a cold, hard shadow trailing behind. I feel warm, faint breath against my forehead. It's crushing me. It's killing me. It's killing its victim.

BEITIRIS REID (11)
City of London Freemen's School, Ashtead Park

THE LIGHTS WENT OUT

The lights went out. I knew it was my friend playing a prank on me. I shouted in destain, 'Annabel!' There was no reply. I repeated it, louder this time. Only silence greeted me. My eyes searched the room but the darkness enveloped me. Tentatively, gathering up my courage, I stepped into the deserted hallway. Every nerve in my body warned me not to continue. I could see a figure ahead of me. He had a sallow, scarred face and the haunted look of someone who had seen many battles. He whispered into my ear softly then he was gone.

TARA GOR (12)
City of London Freemen's School, Ashtead Park

Home Alone

I don't know why being home alone still creeps me. *You're fifteen*, I tell myself, *get over it*. I munch my popcorn and focus on the television. Glancing outside, I notice the snow hasn't stopped. It's been falling for hours and is now at least one foot deep. Suddenly, I see a man through our glass doors. He walks towards the house, a strange smile on his face, a jagged knife in his hand. Heart pounding, I look at the thick snow: he's left no footprints. Then truth dawns. In the glass' reflection I see him behind now me.

Gezana Rai (12)
City of London Freemen's School, Ashtead Park

The Bloody House

Crash! Their car broke down. The two girls exited the car. The rain was pouring, lightning was crashing and they were only wearing short skirts. They saw a cabin in the distance and decided that would be the only place for shelter. After they'd been inside for ages, the lightning still crashing, they could see a figure inspecting their car. *Bang!* There was a thump on the door. They looked out of the window but the figure was gone. They opened the door. A girl with blood dripping from her mouth screamed at them, 'Get out of my house!'

Patrick Crossan (12)
City of London Freemen's School, Ashtead Park

Tap, Tap

I was playing on my phone, texting my brother. We were tapping on the wall to each other, copying the other's tapping pattern. I asked him if I'd woken him and he texted, 'I'm at Grandma's house'. I tapped again but got no answer. I waited until I heard the tap but this time it wasn't on the wall. I slowly peered over my duvet; a darkish figure stood behind the window. He smashed through, my brother's head in his hand. The freakish figure's mask slowly lifted. My daddy was standing there. He said quietly, 'Have a good night's sleep, honey.'

Olly Atkins (13)
City of London Freemen's School, Ashtead Park

Twitch

Why am I up here? I wonder again, shivering, twitching even, as the cold gnaws my bones. The gloomy, decrepit, dilapidated battlements of Hever Castle look far more elevated than they had from down below. My easel creaks and whines in the wind, begging me to retreat back to my cottage. *Twitch*. I drop my brush. Why am I so jittery today? *Twitch*. That's it; I'm leaving this sepulchral place. *Twitch, twitch, twitch*. I'm virtually convulsing now, losing my desperate, fragile grip on reality. I catch sight of something painted on my easel: 'Beware the Twitch!'

William Hart (12)
City of London Freemen's School, Ashtead Park

Alone

The harsh wind howled through the shattered window, dragging in the growl of thunder and its lethal, icy tears. I was usually in my warm, cosy home now, eating a delicious dinner. Unfortunately, I'd lost phone signal in the empty, neglected school so couldn't contact anyone. *Bang!* The door suddenly slammed shut. The last sliver of light left. I heard the click of a lock then saw a dark figure creep into the night. *Hadn't I been alone?* That's what I had thought until the shadows stirred and I felt a cold, blood-stained knife scrape along my bare neck.

Pippa Haslam (12)
City of London Freemen's School, Ashtead Park

The Unknown

I heard a bang and turned round. It was chucking it down, thunder and lightning striking from the dark, gloomy sky. I felt the cold, spooky mist shiver past me. This house hadn't been explored for years; whoever dared enter would never return! I heard a sound upstairs so swiftly went up to investigate. The creaking of the stairs sounded like screeching cats. I approached the room, getting closer by the second. I crept into the room slowly. *Kaboom!* The door locked. Within seconds there was no escape.

Joseph Boros (13)
City of London Freemen's School, Ashtead Park

THE DROP

I sat up, the wind howled as the darkness settled in. I'd just escaped from those devilish tribesmen performing their rituals. I heard a strange mechanical sound in the distance but it was already too late, I was falling. I didn't know how but I was falling down so far. The pain was excruciating as I hit the floor of the cavern. The distance that I fell was impossible to survive. Someone must have wanted to keep me alive; someone who lived so far underground, someone who knew I was coming. That someone now stood right in front of me.

JAKOB WILTON (13)
City of London Freemen's School, Ashtead Park

THE WATCHERS

They are behind you! You don't believe in them but they are always there. They are the cold breath on the back of your neck; the shiver down your spine. When you feel like you're being watched, that's them. When you're walking home late at night, bathed in the murky, yellow streetlight, they are in the shadows. Watching. Waiting. You don't know about them but I do, I know! I've warned many but none have listened, Why don't they listen? But you should because what you don't know is that they've been reading this over your shoulder the whole time!

SHAUNA PUNJABI (12)
City of London Freemen's School, Ashtead Park

The Scream

It was midnight when Lucy heard it: the scream that rang in her ears and echoed around the house. It happened every night but even the top detectives couldn't find answers. She knew the story of Lady Gahala, that someone had murdered her in this house. As the police had installed security cameras, Lucy decided to watch the spare room that night. As she looked at the recordings, Lucy noticed something strange: a face had suddenly appeared. Spooked, she started to go back to bed. All of a sudden she heard a whisper. 'I'll kill you like someone killed me!'

Amelia Rawling (12)
City of London Freemen's School, Ashtead Park

The Tree

The tree has wilted. The baubles on the tree seem like evil grinning faces staring back at me. The air has turned icy cold. I am shivering with fear. It was almost midnight. I was putting the finishing touches to the Christmas decorations before Santa arrived. Suddenly, a crash echoed around the room. The ladder I had been using fell beneath me. I got up, relieved to have survived the fall and looked around. I saw a body, twisted and broken lying under the tree. Now I am here, I realise that it is my body lying under the tree.

Georgie Allan (12)
City of London Freemen's School, Ashtead Park

When I Came Home

I was alone, walking back from school. It was a gloomy night, the sky was coated with an intense layer of fog. The moon was glowing down as I went through the dingy, dark alleyway. As I soon approached my neighbourhood I rang my mum to tell her I would be home soon. She replied with a croaky voice, 'I'll put dinner on.'
Minutes later I walked through the front door, expecting dinner. My mum was nowhere in the house. I shouted out to her, frantically running around searching for her. I looked down, only to see her bloodstained phone.

Amy Field (14)
City of London Freemen's School, Ashtead Park

Peek-A-Boo!

I was playing hide-and-seek with my daughter yesterday. She dashed upstairs in a hurry and proceeded to hide. As I walked up the stairs I heard a giggle coming from the spare room. As I walked in I heard another giggle coming from the cupboard. I opened the cupboard with my eyes shut. I heard her breathing. I said, 'Peek-a-boo, I found you.'
She jumped through the bathroom door and said, 'I win, Mummy. I was in the shower!'

Cameron William Booth Butters (14)
City of London Freemen's School, Ashtead Park

The Dream Man

The Dream Man told me I die at 10.11. I get in my car and start to drive off. I hit a bump. Darn, my tyre's flat. I don't want to get out on this cold, winter evening. It's now 10.05. The car lights flicker on and off. I see someone with long strands of hair in a white rag, their head stooped. The lights flicker. It comes closer, only moving when it's dark. It comes closer. I can't see it anymore. It's 10.10 and it's behind me.

Jamie Young (14)
City of London Freemen's School, Ashtead Park

The Attic

The breeze swept into the attic as I crouched in the corner, an old cloth wrapped around my shoulders. I knew he was coming for me but I didn't move. I don't know why. Looking around the eerily quiet attic was dark and gloomy. I heard a door slam downstairs. I didn't move a muscle, staying as quiet as I could. He was coming upstairs. I knew he would find me. Where to hide? I tiptoed over to the corner of the room, waiting. The eerie sound of the opening door was the last thing I heard...

Helena Le Le Jeune (12)
City of London Freemen's School, Ashtead Park

UNTITLED

I felt like I was being watched. I opened my curtains and froze. There he was, a man sitting in his wheelchair, hands folded, eyes unblinking. Then he was gone, like he'd just disappeared. *What?* I thought to myself, *I swear he was there. Maybe I've just watched too many horror movies*. I sat back down and continued my essay but no, there was that feeling again. And there was the man. Tired of this, I called the police. It turned out the man was dead. One question still haunts me however: who pushed the man from the window?

MARIA RYABINSKAYA (13)
City of London Freemen's School, Ashtead Park

THE HOUSE NEXT DOOR

I'm entering the house now. There's a red liquid dripping from the handle. The door, surprisingly, is open. There's an old mattress with the same red substance staining it. The house seems to be infested with rats. The stairs are in bad condition. At the top of the stairs, looking around, I see no light or signs of life, apart from something that sounds like a hosepipe thumping the ground. There is a lot of red liquid coming from under this door. The smell is absolutely horrific now. I think I can hear movement. I'll ask the person what's happening...

ANDREW SMITH (13)
City of London Freemen's School, Ashtead Park

The Thing

I heard a noise like someone was breaking in. I walked up to the front door and looked out of the eyehole. 'No one was there,' I said to myself. Then as I started walking down the hallway, I heard it again. So I walked up to the door, grabbed the door knob and pulled my door open with frustration. Then I was shocked; there was something that no human could explain. It grabbed me by my throat and threw me to the ground. I ran and I hid in my room then it said, 'I'm coming...'

Davey Fairman
De Stafford School, Caterham

Coming To Play?

'No Mummy, please don't leave me home alone!'
'I will be back soon sweetie.' Her arms clench around me tightly. It had only been two minutes of my mummy leaving then I heard a bang coming from my bedroom. As I slowly creep up the stairs I see that my music box is smashed and on the floor. I freak out and dash for the stairs but trip over painfully at the top and am sent plummeting all the way to the bottom. I hear a high-pitch chuckle coming from the kitchen. 'Mummy?' 'Hahaha.' 'Save me from the monsters, Mummy!'

Josh Waters (12)
De Stafford School, Caterham

The Shopping Trip From Hell

The doors swung open and I stepped in. It felt awfully quiet. With each step the lights started to flicker at me. Then finally the power shut down. I could hear voices in my head... or were they real people? The sound of my heartbeat seemed to echo down the whole aisle, rattling the wine bottles. I turned the corner and suddenly heard a smash. I looked back and saw a shadow block the moonlight. I walked anxiously towards where I saw the strange black shadow. I looked round the corner. A face appeared. I screamed. He stood motionless.

Oliver McCutchen (12)
De Stafford School, Caterham

The Forest Cries

As I walked into the dark, deep and scary forest I heard a loud howl from a pack of wolves. The leaves started rustling behind me. 'Hello? Is anybody here?' I heard the rustling again but louder. I started to get frightened. I looked at my hand. It started to shake. I felt like the tree branches were looking at me. As I began to walk back home I could hear a voice from a distance. It sounded like a girl's voice. It appeared she was saying, 'Help, help me quick.' I turned, a hand touched my shoulder. 'Help, help.'

Olivia Connelly (13)
De Stafford School, Caterham

In The Graveyard

During her lifetime, she had never actually been to a graveyard. The closest she came was holding her breath as the family funeral car drove past. One day when her parents were out, she set off to the nearest graveyard. She was scared as it was 8.30pm. When she arrived the owls hooted and the wolves howled. She cautiously walked around when suddenly one of the gravestones moved and a ghost started chasing her. She yelped and fell, never to be seen again. Her grave lies untouched. No one knows what happened but that's where curiosity gets you, isn't it?

Bethan Allain (12)
De Stafford School, Caterham

Peek-A-Boo!

I hear it, it is over there. I hear it again. It is coming from over there. My feet are cold, my body is severely shaking. As I walk around the floorboards start creaking. There it is again. It is now clearer, getting louder, as if it is now running. The door suddenly slams shut. What am I going to do. My heart is now racing. Then I feel a pale cold hand appear on me. I start to query whether this was such a good idea. I then close my eyes, pray and wish for the best.

Max Roots (12)
De Stafford School, Caterham

THE TAKER

Grasping for her last breath she was taken by the man in the red mask, stolen by the Devil himself. That day Christina had been told to go to Horton's Heath Hotel, despite its legends of a twisted killer. I'd believed it to be a load of codswallop but I was wrong. She went and I didn't warn her. I ran, screaming a dreadful scream. I yelled her name but she was gone. The Devil Man tried to take me but I escaped, leaving Christina trapped. My best friend was gone and it was all my fault. I lost her.

OLIVIA WEBB (14)
De Stafford School, Caterham

DEAD!

I crept into the dark, dusty house. The door screeched closed behind me. I saw a shadow in the corner of my eye but I thought nothing of it so I kept going. I turned back then I felt a cold breeze on the back of my neck. I tried to turn back but a tight grip around my neck shocked me. It got tighter and tighter. I felt a blow to my head then a sharp swipe to my cheek. I tried to shout but couldn't, it was too late. I felt myself fall to the floor!

TORI EDWARDS (11)
De Stafford School, Caterham

Untitled

I was going into the haunted house. I felt nervous. What if I did not come out? As I strolled through, about ten minutes later, I turned to see two men holding knives. I screamed and ran. They cornered me with some painful stabs. I turned onto my stomach to see my blood pouring out of me faster than the wind. I dragged myself across the floor and, as I did, I saw my final seconds. Then came a stab in the head. My life was over.

Amber Worth (11)
De Stafford School, Caterham

She's All Alone...

It was a pitch-black night. Everyone in the family was downstairs. I was all alone. I looked out the window with my head out. I saw something strange. A figure all in black looking straight at me. My head was now all the way out. The figure was as still as a statue. I heard the stairs creaking, the atmosphere that had been loud and happy downstairs was now dead silent. I swung around to look at the door. It opened a little bit. I saw a hand but the door slammed shut. The figure wasn't outside anymore...

Emma Louise Woplin (12)
De Stafford School, Caterham

Jaxon Bloodbay

It was my twelfth birthday and everything was going wrong. My little brother was dying of cancer and my mum and dad told us we were moving. I know people get excited but this house is at 99 Knife Street. It sounded so creepy and that day, on my birthday, we moved. As soon as I got to the house I couldn't move. It was a graveyard! I started walking down the overgrown path. It started pouring and lightning hit a tree. That night I read my book and someone tapped my shoulder. I screamed. Blood went everywhere that night.

Allanna Coghlan (11)
De Stafford School, Caterham

What's Lurking In The Dark?

The shadows formed as the night grew later. I'm in the garden of his house. With the murderer. There is no way out, he trapped me here. It is getting dark, I can hardly see my surroundings. It starts to rain followed by thunder and lightning. I don't even know why I'm here. I don't remember what happened next. I awoke to the noise of dogs barking. I was terrified. I was still tied to the fence. It was still dark outside. A hand untied me and led me to the house. He pulled the trigger, I fell to the ground.

Aimee Banks (13)
De Stafford School, Caterham

What Happens In The Darkness?

The shadow followed us all around the castle but as we stepped out it disappeared. We looked around, we were lost. We looked like misplaced dolls that had been thrown out of a doll's house. We found ourselves in a graveyard and the night was getting dark and gloomy. My friend just wandered off. I heard her scream and gulped. I heard footsteps. I was shivering as they got closer. A hand touched me. They said to me, 'Why did you enter my castle?' I was so scared. The man said to me, 'You will die tonight.'

Ella Hubbard (13)
De Stafford School, Caterham

The Killer

I stepped into the haunted house. My heart was racing. I could hear the wind howling and the building creaking. When I walked up the stairs I heard a scream. I had a little candle with me but it went out. I went towards the room where I heard the scream. I slowly turned the handle. I stopped. The handle had suddenly gone cold like ice. My hand started to shake but I kept on turning. I pushed the door open with a creak and there I saw a black figure with a bloodied dead body on the wooden floor.

Leah Jade Howard (13)
De Stafford School, Caterham

He Is There And Then He Is Not

I saw him, I'm sure I did. I got my phone out and called Danny. 'He's here, come quick!' His black, shadowy cloak hovered in the frosty fog. His hood was covering his mysterious figure. The night was dismal, freeing and gloomy. I strained my back against the dead, lone tree like all the other bodies in this hell-hole. I started hearing eerie whispers from the graves, haunting my mind. It was a flurry; my heart was beating like a rabbit's as it sprinted for its life. I took another peek. He'd vanished. I turned back and felt his presence.

Ben Cunningham
De Stafford School, Caterham

My 'Last' Memory

I'm in a forest. The last thing I can remember is a figure and gunshots. I don't know how I survived. I get up and look around. No sight of anything, just trees. I see a bright, shining light. I move towards it There is nothing around but more trees. Suddenly, I see lots of lights in a row. I follow them. It's a town! I run as fast as I can. I'm there. Lots of people start to get up for the morning. I go up to someone and say hello. They walk right through me... I'm dead.

Travis Drewett (12)
De Stafford School, Caterham

The Forest

It was a dark and stormy night. There was no way out, I was trapped. All I remember was that me and some friends went in the forest and then all I heard was *bang!* I heard screams getting louder and louder. I dropped to the ground. Now here I was, waiting for someone to find me, trying to find a way out. But wait, what was that bright light? Had someone finally found me? 'Hello! Hello! Is someone there? Please! Someone help me! Please, help me!' I began to walk towards the light. I ran faster and faster.

Macie Eden Cotton (13)
De Stafford School, Caterham

No Escape From The Cell

It was deep into the night. Outside the sky was grey, the moon bright in the midnight sky. Bilbo John stood in the icy corridor waiting to be let into his cell. The guard rattled the keys on his belt as he leaned forward to put the large key in the lock. The hairs on the back of his neck stood up. He felt something brush against his skin. In the lock the keys turned loudly and the guard pushed Bilbo into the cell and left. Suddenly, he felt his soul leaving his body as the ghostly figure surrounded him.

Eddie Funnell (13)
De Stafford School, Caterham

The Ramshackle Hut

Fog was creeping across the graveyard like a coffin, closing on the dead. Cautiously, Amy crept towards the ramshackle hut. The graveyard was a frightening death zone. She placed her hand on the icy door and pushed it open. It creaked loudly. The door slammed behind her. She was terrified but she knew it was too late to turn back now. Her footsteps sounded like explosions in the silence. Suddenly, she heard a soft thudding sound. She thought it must be her heart. It started to get louder and louder. Just then she realised it wasn't her. She wasn't alone...

Emily Ffion Edwards (11)
De Stafford School, Caterham

Look Out! Santa's About!

'Ho, ho, ho' were now classed as horrific words after what happened last Christmas. It was so horrific that it wasn't allowed to be mentioned. Now instead of kids getting ready for Christmas, they go under the covers and hid. John was going to bed. It was December the 24th, Christmas Eve. The clock struck twelve and he heard shuffling on the roof. Suddenly, he heard a jingling noise and footsteps slowly coming up the stairs. John quivered and hid in his wardrobe. He heard his door creak open, his parents were working overnight. 'You've been a naughty boy John!'

Samuel Precious (13)
De Stafford School, Caterham

Mystical Shadow

As I walk through the creepy, abandoned woods I find the air around me closing in. I feel them right behind me. I want to scream but it feels like there's something stuck in my throat. I can't breathe. I gasp for air but I breathe nothing in. I feel them crowding behind me, surrounding me, stealing the path before me. I'm trapped in an endless nightmare, there's no way I'm waking up. I need to run. I need to get away. I can't. *My legs*. I'm stuck, I'm scared. Sinking into graves. 'Help! Help!' I scream. 'Too late!'

George Scrase (14)
De Stafford School, Caterham

Screams

I was told to wait in the car. I don't even remember moving. All I remember are the screams, the screams of the wind whistling in the air, the screams of the trees falling to their deaths. It was a chilly and foggy day and as I watched my father entering the emptiness of the dark woods I caught a glimpse of a fast, blurry, moving shadow at the front of our car. The whistling wind grew silent as I sensed the shadow moving closer and closer. Then he whispered, 'Sweet dreams,' and I heard my last screams.

Rhianna Hallett (11)
De Stafford School, Caterham

THE SILHOUETTE

It was a misty night as I was strolling through the haunted town; everything was shredded and abandoned. The only thing guiding me through this nightmare was the gaze of the full moon. *Smash!* The window of the china doll shop shattered and as I suddenly stared sharply at the shop I felt as if the dolls were staring back at me. I looked in front of me and saw a mysterious silhouette of a man holding a chainsaw! I froze! Thunder suddenly clashed! And the man disappeared. I walked towards the ancient gate, opened it slowly and... 'Argh!'

EMILY FINCH (13)
De Stafford School, Caterham

FRANKENSTEIN'S CREATION

Frankenstein created a monster too. His monster wasn't really a monster, he was misunderstood. Perhaps that's true of Lucy also, but that's little comfort when your scream is being gagged by a realistic, child-sized fist being shoved down your throat. I make dolls for extra money and to keep busy on empty widowed nights. I never thought of a doll being like my child until Lucy. Did I wish for her to come to life? I don't know. All I know is I awoke tonight with a beautiful, plastic girl on my chest, stabbing me with a sharp knife.

JAMES KEOGH (13)
De Stafford School, Caterham

The Lonely House

I was walking down a rickety, old path. I saw an abandoned house. All but one window was boarded up and covered in vines and moss. I picked up a rock and threw it through the window. I rushed to the front door. It opened with a creak then slammed behind me. I quickly turned to the door. I tried to open it but it was locked. I heard a creak behind me so slowly turned around. Standing there, in a torn, grey gown, stood a girl with blood dripping from her hands. She lunged right toward me!

Kai Walsh (12)
De Stafford School, Caterham

Abandoned

The empty moon lights up the dismal forest along with the abandoned house. Me and my friends were mindlessly running around the woods, attempting to find an old, abandoned house, home to a barbaric murderer. We came to a halt when my friend Tom spotted something in the distance. We edged closer only to spot the abandoned house. It was engulfed by fog and the door was open. I was pushed in but my friends slowly followed. A small row of hooks hung from the beam supporting the cottage. Then I realised they were bodies on them. He was real!

Christopher Mathers (13)
De Stafford School, Caterham

Ruby?

'Ruby!' I shouted. The wind blew into my face as a shiver ran down my back. 'Ruby? Ruby where are you?' I heard footsteps run up behind me. That's when I started to run. I was running as fast as I could. Was it Ruby? When I looked round my shoulder I saw a face. A face that I hadn't seen before. It was as pale as a blanket of snow. Its hair was as black as coal and its eyes were as bright as the full moon that was out that night. Was it Ruby? It stared at me...

Ellie Gillespie (12)
De Stafford School, Caterham

He's Behind You!

On a dark and gloomy night, Jack was lost in the woods, looking for his dog, Buster. He stumbled on a graveyard and in the misty distance saw an old man hunched over a tombstone. As he cautiously approached him the man raised his hand and pointed to an ancient house. Jack walked towards the unlit house and up the cobweb covered path. The front door was slightly open. Just as he pushed it, he heard yelping from inside and saw Buster hanging from the ceiling. 'No Buster! Who did this?' screamed Jack. An eerie voice answered, 'He's behind you...'

Adam Christoforou (12)
De Stafford School, Caterham

Gone...

It was a glacial day, the sort that ices your heart. It was lashing down pellets. The desolate building stood isolated at the end of an agricultural wasteland. I used the skull-shaped key to unlock the ancient gate. It twisted creakily and the lock snaked away. The gate swung open with a hollow racket. I cautiously crept up the path towards the ever-looming edifice. As I slithered slowly across the weather-beaten tarmac, a shadowy figure emerged from the dilapidated shed. My head turned to face it but it'd mysteriously vanished. 'Hello?' A long, spindly hand slithered over my shoulder.

Charlie Deville (14)
De Stafford School, Caterham

47 Crow Street

I stepped outside of the mansion. I was trying to sell it but no one wanted to buy it. People said that it was creepy. I was about to get into my car but it'd broken down. I guessed I'd have to stay in the mansion and show the people it wasn't that horrible. I went in. It looked very dull; not many lights were on but it'd do for the night. I just got upstairs when I felt something quiet weird. *It's probably cause I'm tired*, I thought. *I'll take a shower.* 'Ahh! Wait! Help!' 'Good night,' it whispered...

Dylan Humphreys (11)
De Stafford School, Caterham

Dark Figure

I saw a figure dressed in black. He had a gun. I kept still while ringing the police. 'Help me, there's a man with a gun.' All of a sudden I dropped the phone as I felt a slither down my back and something pressed against my head. Then I was dragged off screaming. 'Who are you?'
The figure croaked, 'The man of your nightmare.'
Suddenly there was a bang and a pain in my arm; blood oozed out of it. I turned my head to see who it was and what they were doing to my mother.

Sophia McNeil Young (12)
De Stafford School, Caterham

Stalker!

It was the night of Halloween and all the children were partying, except for Angel and Bella, they were going to the deep, dark woods, daring each other to go further. The girls had no idea that a strange man was watching over them from a huge tree. Angel and Bella were getting freaked out by all the creatures that had kept falling on them. Suddenly Bella had gone, she had just disappeared. Angel was getting anxious so she decided to run home. Unfortunately, she was too late. She was stabbed, out of nowhere. These girls were never seen again.

Angel Skilton (11)
De Stafford School, Caterham

Taken

Jack and I were walking our usual route home from school, through the graveyard; the only way to get home. We had a little game we played by ourselves when we walk through the graveyard: who could spot the newest grave.
As we scoured the headstones, the fog started to roll in, making the searching even harder.
'Over here,' called Jack. 'I never knew there was a guy in town with the same name as you.'
He was right, exactly right. It was my name, age and date of birth. Suddenly the ground gave way...

Samuel Vellacott (12)
De Stafford School, Caterham

Into The Woods

One night Katie was walking home when she heard a scream from up ahead. Up ahead was the woods. When people went into the woods they ever come back. Katie didn't know this so she went in. As soon as she entered a man started to follow her. She started to run but couldn't get rid of him. He backed her up against a tree and stabbed her ten times. She collapsed to the floor. Red blood covered her clothes and the leaves on the ground. She was left there to rot. She lies there still.

Kieri-Anais Chapman (11)
De Stafford School, Caterham

Darkness

Darkness drowned me, I couldn't breath. Every step I took seemed meaningless... like me. 'Worthless'? I lived up to it. It used to be like a blanket, the dark. It was comforting, protecting. Now it was like an ocean, swallowing, engulfing me. The tears, the ragged gasps, tugged me further down. I know now that there's no point in struggling, why would I? The more you run, the further you fall, the faster you drown. I don't struggle or fight, I barely breathe. I just wait for death. Slowly, dark, icy grasps set around my neck, my heart. Then... nothing. Darkness.

Katie Copeman (13)
De Stafford School, Caterham

The Unseen Voice

Dark, cold and clammy. 'Hello, is anyone there?' I ask curiously. My words are repeated by an unseen voice. 'Who are you?' I question, terrified. I nervously shuffle backwards, keeping my eyes fixed in front of me. As I keep walking backwards, a cold hand touches my shoulder. A deep voice whispers in my ear, 'I will find you, Dan.' The spine-chilling sentence echoes in my ear constantly. I run. The church bell chimes. I stop. I fall. My eyes can't resist closing. I then realise that a blood trail leads to the grave that I am now lying in.

Nathan Seaman (12)
De Stafford School, Caterham

The Haunted House

One cold and stormy day at the abandoned house, the floorboards were creaking and the doors were slamming. The animals were hiding and the flowers were dying and the forest surrounding the house was as silent as a mouse. A zombie rose from the ground and started to dance to the song 'Thriller'. Everything seemed strange. As I stepped into the house I felt that I wasn't alone. Waves of air shivered through my body. Then a sudden light came from upstairs. My annoying friends were just playing a prank on me so I'm going to get them back!

Jamie Stolton (12)
De Stafford School, Caterham

Dead

I plunged into the darkness of the forest. A bellow echoed through the trees. My footsteps pierced the soundless forest. In the distance lifeless figures blended in with the mist. I ran through the darkness by myself, dodging and weaving past trees. Suddenly, silence. I stopped, motionless; no sound, nothing. As I slowly walked to the nearest street light I looked behind, the figures were gone. I snuck around the cracked bus stop sign. I sat but felt like I was being watched. Before my eyes teenagers in black jumpsuits attacked me and dragged me into the forest. Dead.

Daniel Robinson
De Stafford School, Caterham

The Alone Shadow

I walked along the creaky floorboards Thunder struck and clouds filled the sky with complete darkness. The floor shook dramatically. Blood curdling screams bellowed in my ears. My heart pounded frantically. In the corner of my eye a rusty door awaited me. Cobwebs covered it like a soft, white pillow. I surreptitiously crept towards it, leaning my hand out to reach the dusty handle. Suddenly, a bony, wrinkly hand, as cold as a freezer, was pulling me down. I couldn't breathe. I was going to die! No longer alive. Immediately, I opened my eyes. A shadowy figure awaited me.

Alana Trotter (11)
De Stafford School, Caterham

Graveyard Horror

It was a dark and stormy night. I crept into an abandoned church. It made me shiver as I stood in the fearful church. All I heard were screaming ghosts in the background, very faint. Nearby was a graveyard. *If I go someone might grab me,* I thought to myself, then, *I'm sure I'll be fine,* so I decided to dash outside in a hurry. Someone grabbed me! 'Hello?' I cried but no one was there. I heard this faint sound, it sounded like a doll's song. Suddenly, I heard church bells. I was scared! 'Argh!'

Millie Collins (11)
De Stafford School, Caterham

Rumble

Church is a wonderful place to be, especially when the stained glass windows reflect the sunlight on you, bringing happiness to the world. Tonight we're going to a midnight carol service but I feel something weird is going to happen! I'm at the midnight carol service now and all is going well. Suddenly lightning strikes and screams are let out! I'm starting to panic! *Boom! Crash!* Drastically everyone starts to run but I stay in the church. *Rumble! Rumble!* The ground starts to shake, I'm really scared. Should I run? Bodies erupt from the floorboards. What are they? Zombies!

Lily Funnell
De Stafford School, Caterham

The Thing

Sarah zoomed up the stairs, sensing something was following her. She didn't know what. She didn't care, she just ran. She wanted to look back but knew it was too risky. Whatever was following her made an horrific cacophony. It was like a girl screaming. Sarah stumbled into what she thought was a cobweb but it had an icy touch. Was it a ghost or was it her imagination? When Sarah finally managed to get to the hallway, she discovered an ancient wooden door. She tried to open it but it was locked. Something was waiting for her. But what...

Jessica Grant (13)
De Stafford School, Caterham

A Haunted Night!

It was a cold night, I was walking home from a friend's house in the middle of nowhere. I shrieked, 'I'm lost!' I saw a house and wondered if it was abandoned. Thunder boomed, I screamed. I had to go in. I fiercely walked to the house. The door was half open, I slowly started pulling the door knob. *Crash!* Lightning struck, a window smashed and I jumped to quickly get inside. I ran up the cold, wooden stairs. To my shock I saw a ghost. I fell to the floor, petrified as the ghost haunted over me. 'Help! Help!'

Bella Burns (11)
De Stafford School, Caterham

Lost At Night

Silence, it surrounded me like a swarm of bees. I had suddenly become isolated in the now pitch-black park. Children had run screaming and the sky had thought it was meant to be an eclipse. I sat there, trembling and quivering in the invisible freezer, wishing I could warm myself up. Suddenly, I heard crying from nowhere and a sudden whisper of, 'Joseph.' The fountain of bravery inside me instantly dried up. I couldn't fill it up. I was shaking like a long vibration. 'Why are you scared?' it called again. Sure enough, I knew that voice.

Luke Hagger (12)
De Stafford School, Caterham

TAKEN!

I crept slowly into the abandoned church on a dark and stormy night. My heart was beating vigorously as I heard a piercing scream. I walked into the church, fingers frozen cold. The door slammed shut behind me. I stiffened up. 'Hello,' I cried. No answer. As I shook a candle fell, echoing through the dark church. 'Argh!' I screamed. My back turned, something grabbed me and pushed me over. I scoured the church for any strange creatures. Nothing. Just like a jack-in-the-box A man who was pale and see-through grabbed me. *Whoosh*, I was gone. I screamed!

LILLI MAHER (11)
De Stafford School, Caterham

THE SPOOKY DAY

The dark, gloomy fog surrounded the abandoned house. I was tempted to go in. Finally I bravely walked into the house. Dust flew into the air frighteningly. I heard horrifying noises from a short distance. A door slammed loud behind me. I tried to escape quickly but the door was locked. Then out of the blue the lights turned off. Tears were flowing from my eyes as quick as lightning. I turned around to see the most terrifying thing in the world. A red, ferocious monster. I shut my eyes and opened them again. I jumped. It was all a dream.

KYLE SINGH (11)
De Stafford School, Caterham

Ghost Girl

The wind howling, Lucy walks past the churchyard in fear. Waiting for her friends in the cold, damp, empty church. She hears noises from under the floorboards, no one in sight. It's dark, the only light was coming from the moon, shining in the stain glass window. The clock ticking whilst she's shaking in fear. *Bang!* She looks to see what it was. All she can see is an empty church. Lucy had been there for a long time. Her friends didn't turn up. She does have one friend in there though, but not a human friend!

Alex Sharp (12)
De Stafford School, Caterham

The House

The forest was covered in a thick blanket of darkness. Deep in the forest was a grand house that had rumours to the name. Only few were brave enough to enter but little did they know of the fate that awaited them. For inside lurked a faceless figure that murdered his victims and sent their bodies back to the town chopped up into tiny pieces. Around the property was a circle, a circle of blood, that was painted with their hearts. In the garden of the house were their heads which laid upon spikes.

Harry Ramsey (14)
De Stafford School, Caterham

Lake House

I was wandering through the black forest. I only had my thoughts. There was a lake. Suddenly, a bridge appeared. It went along the water to a big, creaky house with blacked out windows, wooden boards mostly fallen off. Terrifyingly, the bridge I had walked across to get to the house vanished. I walked up to the door. It creaked open. I pushed it and walked inside but then it slammed behind me and I heard a spine-chilling scream. I pulled the door as hard as I could but it was no use...

Becky Matlock (12)
De Stafford School, Caterham

Unknown

As I walk through the ghostly town, the fog weaves its way through the buildings. Cautiously, I dip my hand in the running waterfall, wondering what treasures lay under the water. I can see an abandoned hotel. As I head towards it I hear the chiming of bells. My eyes instantly stare at the church. However, the bells are not moving. Running to the hotel, I hear a bang. My body shivers. I reach for the ancient door handle. The door creaks open. Hesitating, I step inside. I see a black figure. I decide to chase it. Big mistake...

Emmie Mai Paxton (13)
De Stafford School, Caterham

The Man In The Mask

Smack! He pressed me against the glass. It left a bloody mark. He still wore that terrifying mask. It was so dark outside. The louder I bellowed, the more he would cut. *Slit. Drip. Drop. Drip. Drop*. A puddle was forming. *Drip. Drop. Drip. Drop.* The red liquid flowed from my arm like a river. *Slit*. Another cut was made*. Drip. Drop. Drip. Drop*. I was paralysed. Salty tears dripped down my pale cheek. 'I have had enough!' I screeched at the top of my voice. 'You're scaring me. Stop! I hate you!' He made one last cut. *Drip. Drop.*

Millie Bonas (12)
De Stafford School, Caterham

The Dark

I crept carefree down the foggy street. The fog started to blind my eyes but I'd noticed a dark silhouette of a man carrying a heavy looking object in his hand. I ran to the closest place; it was a church. I slammed the dusty door shut. The lights automatically turned on. The church was plastered with cobwebs, they covered the stained glass windows. It looked like an abandoned house. 'Hello?' I said. The lights turned out. *Bang! Smash! Crack!* Everything was gone. 'Who's there?' I questioned. The lights turned on! 'Argh!' I screamed, then turned. He was there!

Paris Dell
De Stafford School, Caterham

Slither

I stop. A paralysing snake crawls up my spine from the inside. I can't move. I can't breathe. I feel the flesh fall off my legs and arms: killing me slowly, in agony. It shivers across my face. I try to claw it off but I can't. Then it slides back down my spine to feast on my insides. I can't escape. Gusts of frosty wind engulf me. I fall to the floor, grating my fingertips on the cobblestones in desperation. My only real danger is clear to see, I could never conceal the depression in me.

Katie Spurgin (12)
De Stafford School, Caterham

Breath Of Death

It was getting dark. The cold, frosty night crept in on James like a lion stalking its prey. His mum wasn't back but he was tired so he decided to go up for night. Suddenly, a creak then a thump came from upstairs. James listened. *It's just my brother*, he thought. James proceeded cautiously. *Thump*. 'Ahh!'
'It's alright Harry, I'm coming!' he said in a motherly voice. He flung open the door. Harry wasn't there! There was a deafening slam as the window flew off its rusty hinges. James looked out. He felt cold, wet breath on his neck. 'Mum?'

Ross Lever (12)
De Stafford School, Caterham

The Hand

I felt the heat of the evil when I entered the tormented house. I cautiously walked through the crooked door. As I went through I felt heat as if a scorching hand was touching my back. I picked up the pace. I tried to be quiet in case the monster didn't know I was there. Suddenly the lights dimmed. My heart went faster. I heard a voice from behind, 'Stop and wait or else...' I turned around, A large man stared at me, his big hands banged down on my shoulder, my beating heart rate went faster.

Ella-Daisy Spurgeon (13)
De Stafford School, Caterham

Shadows

The man cautiously stepped into the dark forest as the sweat dripped from his forehead. The moonlight was slightly visible through the thick leaves on the trees. Figures rustled through the bushes top either side of him. He stopped and trembled in fear as a tall, dark figure with gleaming red eyes emerged. The figure slowly moved towards the man like a snake slithering towards its prey. The cold air chilled the man's back. He tried to move his legs but was in so much shock he couldn't. The man closed his eyes. Everything went black.

Reuben Hart (12)
De Stafford School, Caterham

One Breath

Don't breathe, he'll hear. Can you hear your heart? He can hear it too. Do you hear the thump of boots against the worn floorboards? He's creeping closer yet it's the spine-chilling echoes that really terrify you. You can't get them out of your head, can you? I couldn't. Close your eyes and hide in the darkness. He'll find you though, he never fails to. You sit there, paralysed with suffocating fear, dreading your undeniable death. Oh, you believed in escape? I'm sorry. You won't be the first or the last; I'm evidence of that. Wait! Did you just breathe?

Leila Treacher (13)
De Stafford School, Caterham

The Forest

Thump. The very Earth shook with tremors. *Thump*. The fog weaved itself around the trees. *Thump*. It was getting closer by the second. *Thump*. I could feel cold sweat snaking down my spine. *Thump*. Patches of moonlight were visible between the gaps in the trees. *Thump*. The rough, hard bark dug into my back. *Thump*. The night air was cold and getting steadily colder as it approached. *Thump*. My breath fogged the chilly air. *Thump*. I could feel my heart hammering in my chest. *Thump*. My breath quickened. *Thump*. There was a terrifying roar. *Thump*. It was here at last...

Allan Jacob (12)
De Stafford School, Caterham

THE FOE

I stumbled down the pathway, noises coming from left and right. I knew I wasn't going to make it there, knew I wasn't going to get to the antique church in time. As I lumbered down the dirt track I saw sanctuary: a small shack of the darkest oak wood. I was sprinting now. Just to reach that refuge would mean the world. I edged closer and closer. Only ten metres to go. One foot after the other. The footsteps behind got louder and louder. Just five metres to go. The stomping came like screams. *Thud*. My foe was waiting.

PAIGE CASH (12)
De Stafford School, Caterham

THE CREEPY CHURCHYARD

The wind pushing against my face, I gingerly walked through the churchyard. The crumbling of the gravestones filling my ears. I could feel the arms of fear strangling me. All went silent. Then a loud scream echoed through the air. I turned around. All of a sudden, I felt a bony hand grip my ankle. Tossing and turning, sweat running down my forehead as fingers slowly dug into my skin. I screamed, getting louder and louder! My heart skipped a beat. Tears rolling down my red, rosy cheeks. My eyes opening slowly. I woke up, feeling relieved.

LEAH CARDY (11)
De Stafford School, Caterham

Nightmare

One dark, spooky night Lisa was walking aimlessly through the forest. The skinny dead trees stared into her soul. Crows screeched loudly, the wind vigorously blew the dead, brown leaves. The sky was like ink leaking onto the scenery. Her heart started racing faster and faster. Then suddenly, Lisa heard a loud, high-pitched girl's scream. She panicked and started to sprint wildly, helplessly. *Why did I decide to explore?* she thought. Then she staggered and fell over a large twig as someone's sweaty hands covered her mouth. The last thing she heard was, 'Bye-bye.' *Crack*. Her neck broke.

Sacha Eden
De Stafford School, Caterham

Untitled

Small wisps of floating cobwebs entwine around my ankles, chilling my feet through the woven holes of my socks. I stiffly walk forward, gazing into the oblivion of darkness ahead. The only light that remains is the flickering candle in my hand that also seems to be quivering in fear of the eerie, silent tension that fills the air. My footsteps echo and creak on the wooden floorboards as they bend beneath me. The room temperature quickly drops. The candle's immediately extinguished. I hear breathing, firm and heavy in the cold air. A hand lands on my shoulder.

Charlotte Eleanor Vicars (14)
De Stafford School, Caterham

THE SHADOW

The moon shines brightly over the deserted moors. Swampy land bubble with gas. Crows caw and winds roar. Welcome to Cackle Street.
The higgledy-piggledy silhouettes of houses are illuminated by the moon. The pitter-patter of raindrops are dancing fairies upon the road. A young teenage girl is meandering down the cursed lane; a stray dog who doesn't have a destination. She answers to 'Lola'. She wanders around at midnight, listening to the music of wolves. She lurks in shadows, waiting to pounce; a predator on the hunt. Her presence, a weight on everybody's shoulders; even yours.

AVA KARANTH (12)
De Stafford School, Caterham

DARKNESS

I turned around. The darkness engulfed me, making me a part of it. I couldn't see my hands. My eyes blurred (were they open or closed?) I tried to scream but my throat was blocked. How many days had I been in this musty darkness? I started to crawl in what I hoped was an easterly direction. As I shuffled along, my hands touched something wooden. I reached up, finding a metal fixture. Sending shivers down my spine, I grasped it, turned it, and waited for the click of the lock telling me I was doomed. Then light poured in...

NATHAN KILLICK (12)
De Stafford School, Caterham

The Missing Girl

It was one of those typical dark, rainy nights again. Well, that's what I thought at the time. I was staying at my friend, Ashley's, house over night. There was no one else in the house apart from us. We were sitting in her room watching a film when we heard a noise. Nothing was there. It kept on happening but it could have just been the wind. Ashley said she was going down into her basement. Ten minutes later she hadn't back. She never did. Where did she go? What happene? No one knows...

Imogen Carter (13)
De Stafford School, Caterham

Carousel Horse

I walked towards the supposedly haunted funfair. The soggy grass was clingibg onto my shoe for its life. The cold wind blew an old piece of cloth that covered a carousel horse; my skin turned ice cold at the sight of red liquid splattered on its face. I screamed and ran towards the exit. As I ran I tripped over a decaying rabbit. Tears streamed down my face as I crawled away from the dead rabbit. As I backed away I felt something sharp touch my back. A hand touched my shoulder. A voice boomed, saying, 'Hello, darling.'

Skye Friend (12)
De Stafford School, Caterham

The Man Behind Me

As I was walking through the darkened woods, I heard mysterious music from a deserted house. I had never heard this kind of music before. So I decided to investigate. As I crept up the creaky path I saw a tall, hump-backed figure. He looked familiar. I pressed the doorbell and felt myself fall. When I finally woke up I looked around the haunted room. I could see a door but was too scared to open it. All of a sudden I felt a deep breath on my frozen neck. I turned around and there in front of me was...

Katie Groves (13)
De Stafford School, Caterham

Go Into The Woods

The wood is a place where I used to love to go to. I went to the woods where whispering and voices were close to me. A shudder of fear and cold went down my spine as I ran away from home and to reach freedom, only this wasn't the right direction. Something brushed past me. I turned around, there was nothing there. My heart was thumping louder than ever. 'You're not meant to be here,' a voice whispered. I fell to the ground with fear. The woods surrounded me with the lurking dead. After that I was not known as the same.

Stesy Pesce (13)
De Stafford School, Caterham

Spiders

One Friday morning, the 13th of November, the king I woke up. I heard a bloodcurdling scream which broke the silence of the graveyard. I got up to investigate. Slowly I got up from my blood-stained pillow then I in my parent's room, as I stepped into the master bedroom I realised something was wrong. I grasped the rough duvet of my mother's bed... a skeleton lay there, cold and undisturbed. Something had gone terribly wrong. I looked around and I found a gigantic spider staring at me, ready to pounce.

Reuben Lucas Medhurst (12)
De Stafford School, Caterham

Footsteps

I sullenly walked through the graveyard, shuddering at the very thought of disintegrated corpses laying beneath my feet. Lightning struck down around me and thunder shook the earth like a pounding drum. I shrieked, running for the nearest shelter: a neglected house that was almost a pile of rubble. As I entered the house, I heard a creak, then swift footsteps coming towards me. I froze in terror, hardly, daring to breathe. A pale, white hand crept out of the shadows and followed by it a cadaverous deathly white face. Looming out of the gloom grinning at me, laughing mockingly.

Kiara Kielkiewicz (11)
De Stafford School, Caterham

By The Graveyard

By the graveyard, it's daunting, at midnight you hear a bell ring, it's just your imagination you say to yourself... until you look outside. You live near the graveyard, it's pitch-black. What's that you see? A figure appears in the shadows, it doesn't look like a human form. Your mind is racing and getting confused and you're scared to know what it is. You open your window and shine a torch where you could see the figure. But there is no shadow, no shape, you return to your bed as a shadow follows across the wall.

Elliot Ruddock (11)
De Stafford School, Caterham

The Dripping Noise

It's late at night and I'm in bed. I can hear a really weird dripping noise. I ignored it but now it has become really annoying so I'm getting up. I don't bother putting the lights on and I fiddle with the taps in the bathroom. I get back into bed but the noise is back so I go into the bathroom and turn on the lights. It was the shower... with blood dripping out. I panic and turn around. There is a clown looking at me. I scream and run out of the house. But where can I go?

Amy Lou Wilsher (11)
De Stafford School, Caterham

I'M COMING!

Rubbing his hand down the old, rusty gate, he called. 'Jack are you coming?' He walks inside the ancient church, the mist rolling beneath his eyes. He runs inside and jumps in the pulpit hugging his legs. He hears the door with a mighty screech! Michael, trying not to cry, the footsteps running along the old church floor.
'Where are you?' Michael, trying not to reply, footsteps getting closer and closer and then everything stops. Michael's not sure what to do, hugging his legs like his life depended on whether to get up or to stay down, really scared, he stands and...

JOSHUA HEATH (11)
De Stafford School, Caterham

LOST

It was a chilly and foggy evening and as I was running through an abandoned forest... when I tripped. I could see the creature getting closer... I cried. It was emerging from the fog, I got up, slipping as I sprinted off. Looking for somewhere to hide amongst the trees, I found a rusty key on the ground and shoved it in my pocket. Then I found a house, I tried the key and shoved it in the door. It creaked as I stepped inside. I tried to find my phone, when suddenly the figure appeared and grabbed me.

GIGI FRENCH (12)
De Stafford School, Caterham

The Blood Apple

Lightning struck the forest floor as rain began to settle on the spiked leaves of the trees. One apple plummeted to its death from the home of its cursed tree. Whoever plucked the apple from its spot would be promised a slow, painful death. This was the blood apple. The curse upon this apple was called the chattering skulls. It was called this because the one who picks it was then cursed and the result of this is that the temperature of your body would plummet. But then, the apple was plucked. Their insides were beginning to freeze up. Dead.

Thea Alsleben (12)
De Stafford School, Caterham

Rampage

A cold drifting fog crept in my car and moaned the silent night with a painful prick of my finger. My brain tells me that I am in pain, I look down to see the scattered glass over my arm and lap. Even though I know I am in danger, my brain tells me to stay calm. The fog starts getting thicker and fills my lungs as I notice the orange flames dancing around me. Suddenly, a loud but dismal laugh creeps its way into my ears.

Tom James Taylor (14)
De Stafford School, Caterham

The Grave Within

The grave within holds everybody, haunting who least expects it. It creeps and crawls from body to brain, making little kids insane. No one know who will fear its wrath. Its devilish hell, its ferocious bite. The bite burrows fear within. Whoever is bitten by the grave within will see their fears within. The darkest, deepest ones they have that no one's ever seen. The fears lurk out into the brain at night. Why? Because it fears daylight. If they lurk out into daylight they will rot and burn. Whoever dares to read is its next hopeless, innocent, scared victim!

Ben Bradshaw (11)
De Stafford School, Caterham

The Hunted

Crouched in the corner of my cell, hearing other inmates being tortured by guards. Sometimes I think the world has forgotten me. Guards never come down to my cell, maybe the last inmate was killed down the corridor where my cell is. The guards act strange around me like I am a ghost. I was once a free man as all people are but someone came on my private property and threatened to kill my children, that was it. I killed a man, I remember that day so well, I have nightmares about it.

Toby Burton (12)
De Stafford School, Caterham

THE CHURCH

The rain was now getting heavier, the wind was howling down this dark, misty alleyway. I saw a church up ahead, I ran, I could always wait there for Harry. I felt a shiver go down my spine and a tickle on my neck. I shouted, 'Harry? Harry, is that you?' All of a sudden I heard a scream echo through the church. I shouted for Harry one last time. Then I saw a shadow hover above me. I screamed...

SOPHIE JONES (12)
De Stafford School, Caterham

CHASE

I was in the forest with Zac and Max when we came across a dark, mysterious figure. Max was scared but Zac said, 'Come on.' We crept towards it as it crept towards us. Suddenly we were face to face with the mysterious figure.The frightening monster lifted up his hood and revealed a grizzly, horrible green alien with slime dripping from its mouth. We ran and ran, he had tripped up on some roots. The monster had abducted Zac. Max and I panicked, we did not realise until it was too late.

DOM MCCARTHY-KING (13)
De Stafford School, Caterham

The Stormy Night

One time there was a girl who went for a walk. Suddenly it started to rain and storm so she looked for shelter. All she could find was an abandoned house in the woods. She crept in and went down the hallway. Suddenly, the door slammed behind her and she heard a voice behind her saying, 'Leave.' She was scared out of her mind. She started screaming, ran back down the hallway, slammed open the door and ran out into the stormy hail. She sprinted back to her nice, warm house, never to return again.

Daniel Higgins (12)
De Stafford School, Caterham

Have A Look

So, there're monsters in the closet you got your dad to close? Well, what makes you think monsters can't open doors? I was brave. I opened the door. Big mistake. A pale, white figure grabbed my hair and pulled me in. Shivers ran down my spine. The hairs on my neck stood up. I cried but nobody could hear my echoing screams. Its dagger teeth bit me on the arm. I fainted. I woke in a bright, white room. Wires were in my arms, my blood running through them, draining me alive. I grabbed a blade, ready to end everything.

Eleanor Heasman (13)
De Stafford School, Caterham

Abigail's Alleyway

As I walked down the deserted alley, I trembled with every step. I had always ignored the tales of Abigail but today I wondered if they were true even thought I'd convinced myself they were just stories to scare you. I heard movement. 'Hello?' I called out. The only response was a high-pitched scream. As I turned around the corner, I felt an icy hand grab me from behind. It was then that I realised the truth. I knew then I was wrong: Abigail was real and I was next.

Charlotte Borman (13)
De Stafford School, Caterham

Man

Thunder filled the air with shrieks and squeals. A gruesome man lay sleeping in the graveyard, his entwined dreadlocks hanging off a rotten bench. His eyes were crimson, they curdled your blood with fear. A lonely boy came strolling past, homeless and abandoned. He asked every person if they could help. Well, *this* person might have been a mistake. Slowly creeping up to him the boy said in a quiet voice, 'Could I have some money?' The boy stood in fear of what was happening in front of him. The sound of the boy's snapping bones was revolting.

Liam Jones (13)
De Stafford School, Caterham

I Watched...

Right then I knew what was going to happen. Her sunken eyes melted, streams running down her paper-thin cheeks. Her body shook and her arm rose, holding a gun that shone brightly in the moonlight. Her cold, blue eyes didn't shine like they used to. I wanted to run, to escape, and pretend this was a dream. I thought about the things we had done together, the memories sparkled like stars in my mind. The seconds felt like hours as I stood silently, in full control of what was to happen. *Click.* I watched death. I watched her fall.

Charis Faulkner (13)
De Stafford School, Caterham

The Voice

There were rumours, rumours about a lady. An old one at that. According to Lauren's friends she was spotted in the woods from dusk till sunrise. Lauren reckoned they were lying but at dusk she went to check it out. Just to make sure. Quiet whispers flowed around the woods. Lauren checked over her shoulder but nobody was there. She was about to head home when she heard a drip. The blood formed a puddle. Blood filled the mud and Lauren ran. Her friend, Alice, was dead, soundless on the floor. 'Hello, little one,' came an old, gentle voice.

Zachary Jennings (12)
De Stafford School, Caterham

Memorable Faces

I awoke from my slumber to an ominous whisper. I leaped from my bed into the bitter winter breeze. A whistling shiver fell down my spine, raising the hairs on the back of my neck. I slowly peeked under my bed, yet to my relief there was nothing to be found, As I arose I felt an unwanted presence. How could such a memorable face be so obscure? All the same familiar features yet the passion I once felt towards him was there no more. Once he had eyes of sapphires now only eyes of nothingness. How could I forget?

Amber Dabin (13)
De Stafford School, Caterham

Killer Clown

As I left for work I felt a strange chill down my back, like I was being watched. By the time I got back I could still feel the chill. I went outside to see what was out there. This morning I'd seen something like a hatch. When I went to look it turned out my eyes hadn't deceive me; there was a hatch and from the look of it it came from WWII. In the far corner I saw a mask, a clown mask. That night I heard an intruder. It was the clown.

Liam Gibson-Quinn (13)
De Stafford School, Caterham

The Scare

As I sat on the fragile, ancient stool I felt my heart beating out of my chest. Quick shivers regularly crawled down my delicate spine. I was disorientated. I suddenly heard a loud scream. This was no ordinary scream. This was a deadly scream. I slowly crept towards where the scream came from. I heard a slow drip landing on the cold floor. I then grasped my hand around the door that was shut to. I peered my head around the corner. I then saw an image that I would never get out of my mind. My chest exploded!

Courtney-May Colburn (12)
De Stafford School, Caterham

Untitled

Have you ever thought about, once you've switch off the lights, what lurks there? When you stare into the unknown, when you hear strange noises? You say to yourself, 'It's just a figment of my imagination.' Well, how do you know that? Have you ever gone to your window? Have you checked behind the curtains? Have you opened your closet? I don't think you have. You just go to sleep every night when you climb into bed, your brain recharging; up go the senses and your eyes black out. That's when a certain happening occurs.

Jimi Bristow (14)
De Stafford School, Caterham

Hell's Graveyard

Ancient fog filled the midnight breeze. No one dared to come here. I thought it was a joke. I should have known my fate. I charged in the unknown, walked into a circle with graves around me, when suddenly the ground was pulled away. It turned into Hell! Swiftly hands came up from the earth. I was scared to death. Then cold, thick breath began breathing on the back of my neck. That's when I realised the army of dead were around me. They started to drag me to the bottomless fiery depths of Hell.

Stanley Salmon (11)
De Stafford School, Caterham

On My Way To School

I walked to school every morning, even in winter. The streets get darker but still I walk alone. It's silent. Only my footsteps can be heard and the drops of rain on my coat. No one is seen, not ever... not until this morning. I could sense someone following me but when I turned, nobody was there. I was baffled, petrified. I was halfway to school and I wasn't alone. I could feel them, waiting to pounce. I never made it to school that day. Instead I was left for dead in a forest. Now I'm ready for my revenge...

Imogen Grace Oxley (13)
De Stafford School, Caterham

The End Is Near!

It hit me. The end was coming. It was all over now. The screaming, the shouting, it's stopped because everyone's gone. Dead! He'd haunted us for an excruciating amount of time and we'd had enough. I won't let him capture me, not like the rest. He threatened us, took away our families, everything we had until we had nothing; I have nothing! It's just me left now, just me and him, but I won't give up, I will keep running, keep hiding. I'm afraid that no one can escape his shadow. Here he is, it's coming and he's not stopping.

Amy Ledger (13)
De Stafford School, Caterham

The Unknown

The darkness is suffocating. I sit still, shivering. My senses deluded, the smell of damp invades my nostrils. Unable to see my surroundings, I feel around. Icy tiles cut my quivering palms. My back's tense against the wall's corners. My blood's numbing my veins. The coldness spreads. Suddenly, I'm sent into a panic. My heart races as I struggle to remember how I got her, who I was. Muffled mumblings, deep in tone, echo down toward my shivering body. Plunging into hysteria, I begin to panic. Footsteps. *Creak*. There's a shard of light. I'm in a basement. The door opens...

Georgia Pitts (13)
De Stafford School, Caterham

Death...

How do you know when it's over? When do you know your time's up? They say your life flashes before you in a few seconds but to me that doesn't seem fair: all those years of living and making memories, over in the blink of an eye. What if time froze and you got to relive your favourite moments or watch them back as if they were on TV? I suppose if everyone did that people would look forward to death and that's not what death is. Death is depressing, death is pain, death is lonely... I should know.

Alice Forde (13)
De Stafford School, Caterham

The Silhouette

Every day there is someone, some*thing* that lurks behind you. The dark silhouette leaves nameless footsteps. Your head becomes restricted. Your name will be called but you won't know who called it. It's him. A small breeze would brush past your hairs, creating shivers through your body. High-pitched tones will vibrate your ears, leaving a heart wrenching panic which suffocates your body. He may be out of sight but he will never leave your side. Even when he buries you in your grave.

Molly Arnold (13)
De Stafford School, Caterham

At The End Of The Bed...

No one was awake, you could only hear the heavy sleeping of Polly, the oldest sibling. She was in a very deep sleep and was having a frightful nightmare. In her nightmare there was a clown that would go around murdering people who dreamt about him. After about fifteen minutes of claiming this awful dream, she woke up with a sudden scream. She had been a victim of the clowns and woke up because of this. Polly realised something at the end of her bed. It was the clown from her nightmare. A scream broke the silence of the house.

Collette Marie Cardy (14)
De Stafford School, Caterham

I'll Write Tomorrow

Dear diary, it happened again today. My reflection stayed, staring. Just like on Friday in the school toilet's mirror. It's always an older version of me. My skin wrinkly with a pasty complexion and a placid soul. The ripples in the water send shivers down my spine. The creepy thing is, every time I catch it, my reflection's closer to the surface. I can't avoid it, fear bubbles in my stomach with every glimpse of that emotionless face. I'm scared to look in a mirror or any kind of liquid. I have to go, I'll write tomorrow. My bath is ready.

Skye Sidwell (13)
De Stafford School, Caterham

Nightmare Come True

As the temperature dropped like a wintry breeze, we both knew we shouldn't have trespassed. She looked from shoulder to shoulder as something replaced her soul with theirs, lifting her into midair. I wanted to help her but I was too busy being paralysed by fear. When I woke up I was relieved to find out it was only a dream! However, goosebumps shot up on my arms as I felt the sensation of being watched. I looked to one side and there she was, staring blankly at me. I couldn't move, I really was paralysed with fear after all.

Sky Angel Mackie (13)
De Stafford School, Caterham

The Child

It was a dark, stormy night and his mum had arrived home. She shouted to her son and husband, saying, 'I'm home!' There was an eerie silence. Silence so tense you could cut it with a knife. Hearing no response, she made her way up to the bedroom only to find her son, chunks of flesh hanging from his hands. Blood poured from the body which lay below the boy. A child's laugh should not be so evil... so monstrous. His smile was plastered across his face. She knew he had problems but not that bad. Dad lost the game.

Jessica Owen (14)
De Stafford School, Caterham

Footsteps

Thump, thump, thump, thump. My heart won't stop racing. Cold, sharp sweat droplets fall continuously down my forehead. I'm trapped, in danger, why won't someone just come and save me now? I swear I can hear the deadly echoes of footsteps making their way closer and closer. My shaky, heavy breathing is the only thing filling in the morbid silence... except for those haunting footsteps which are longing to find me. I can't move, I just can't. The fear has taken over my weak body. *Tap, tap.* The footsteps are getting louder, my heartbeat faster. Nothing can help me now.

Jenna Flood (14)
De Stafford School, Caterham

The House At The End Of The Road

I was walking to the house at the end of the road where nobody goes, trying not to show any fear. I was now standing at the front of the black door. I walked up to the cold steps. When I walked to the door it opened with a creak. Nervously, I strolled in slowly. All that was in front of me was a staircase, no lights were on and I could see nothing. Suddenly the door slammed shut and I was in complete darkness. I could feel my cold breath and a cold hand reached out and grabbed me.

Amber O'Donoghue (12)
De Stafford School, Caterham

Ownership

I lay on my bed, almost falling asleep. I couldn't move but didn't know why. Pressure pushed onto my chest with almighty force. I was unable to breathe. I lay helpless and still, pinned to my bed. The immense weight was crushing. I feared for my life. Harsh, icy breath affected my inner sanity. Suddenly, the sound of a crushing rib penetrated my ear drum. Sweat dripping from my brow, my body trembled. A frozen hand engulfed my face. Trepidation took over my inner thoughts, my soul now defeated by the entity that had entered my room and taken over.

Christopher Box (13)
De Stafford School, Caterham

Ricky?

We thought exploring the forest in daylight was okay. Until Ricky went missing. Shouting his name, we stumbled across an old and rickety house. Inside, a deadly scream echoed. A chill ran down my spine as I anxiously called out his name into the darkness. I heard laughing from upstairs. 'I'm up here!' he shouted. I laughed before I began climbing the steep stairs. That is, until a hand closed around my wrist and I looked down to see Ricky by the stairs. 'Don't,' he whispered, his eyes wide with fear.

Faye Daniels (13)
De Stafford School, Caterham

Aghast

The room was pitch black apart from one mere candle in the centre, flickering in the light breeze that came from the slightly open window. I held my freezing hands near the candle trying to warm them. Without warning, a great gust of wind pounded the single-glazed window and it rattled, almost shattering. I heard a deep, faint, low-pitched voice call out my name in the distance. I shivered. *Thud, thud, thud.* Something was coming. I crept into the corner and hid behind a crate. I glanced over and there, on the wall, was a ghastly shadow.

Fardeen Dowlut (13)
De Stafford School, Caterham

The Abandoned House

Across the road from 12 Hairwood Drive, is an old abandoned house. No one ever steps foot in there, my neighbour says apparently it is haunted. Every night two red eyes glare out of the window. Every evening I try and force myself to go over there. It took me three months but eventually I went there and climbed through the hole in the front door of the abandoned house. I stepped inside and had one foot on the bottom step and a strong breeze swiped me off my feet. Two bloody hands dragged me up the stairs.

Jessica Stanley (14)
De Stafford School, Caterham

The Baby Monitor

David had just come home from a day at work. He had picked up his little daughter and had just settled her down for the night. His wife, Jane, was still at work as she leaves late. David went straight to bed and needed to sleep off a long, hard, depressing day.
After a while, David heard the monitor. The baby's crying, but realised that Jane was singing a lullaby, 'Go to sleep.' Before dropping off again he heard a muffling noise in the wardrobe. It's Jane tied up in rope. Then the monitor roared with loud screams.

Ross Wilsher (14)
De Stafford School, Caterham

The House!

Ominously, the sky darkened, dismally creating violent shadows on the sidewalk. Before the young boy, stood a tall and proud house.
It was old and decaying but looked as if it were the only thing of importance in the area. Standing lonely and isolated deathly voices in the wind that swooped past the crippled trees echoed inside him. As he approached the house, the door creaked open with the haunting silence of suspense pushing him in. Without fully realising what was happening, he helplessly fell to the cold marble floor. What was this place he had woken up in?

Molly Dunnett (11)
De Stafford School, Caterham

Voices In The Woods

Mia stomped through the dark, eerie wood. Rain thrashed her head and body. Suddenly, the forest floor fell to silence. An ear-piercing screech echoed around the forest. Mia pleaded for it to stop. After hours of pleading everything stopped! Clown-like figures bounced from tree to tree singing, 'You did it, you did it, we all know that you did it.' Mia screamed in pain, she didn't mean to do it. It just happened. Mia spun and swirled, trying to keep them all in eye contact. In the end, all that was left was a pile of clothes.

Isabel Ankers (12)
De Stafford School, Caterham

Ghost Stories

Tiptoe up the stairs so as to not wake anyone up. Open the creaky door. Go to turn on the light. A cold, damp draft shivers down your spine. You look inside. A pair of glaring eyes! You turn around, a hand lands on your shoulder. You run downstairs, the ceiling starts closing in, sweat drops down your forehead. The walls and ceiling turn to mirrors, there is no way out. The walls start closing in. You feel dizzy, you spin round; ghosts are all around you. The room is on fire, you drop to the floor.

Matthew Major (11)
De Stafford School, Caterham

Falling!

I walked through the woods on my way home from school. Suddenly I heard a scream. I said to myself, 'Breathe, it's OK!' But was I too late? After that I started to run but I fell. I fell down a scary, dark, black hole. I couldn't see the bottom. A few seconds later, which felt like ten minutes, I shivered with fear as I landed on a cold, stiff body. As I turned round I saw someone else falling but it looked like someone I knew! Was it someone from school? My alarm rang and I woke in fear!

Lillie McCarthy King (11)
De Stafford School, Caterham

Archaeologists In A Tomb

After many years of digging and searching, my archaeologist friends and I finally found a secret doorway to a long lost Egyptian pyramid. We pushed the main stone out of the way and decided to explore the tomb. Walking around, we discovered the burial place of an Egyptian pharaoh. There were a set of bones lying beside the tomb. Someone said they looked like the bones of a large dog. Interested, we began to search the place when suddenly, a soft growl came from behind us. It was a huge hideous dog, it had come to life and was prepared to kill someone!

Daniel Clarke (13)
De Stafford School, Caterham

Possession

I felt the weight on my back, nails under my skin. Somewhere between awake and dreaming. I lay helpless, motionless, yet my mind was screaming. I fought against the power of a stallion, it pinned me down; pressure so cold forced its way into my lungs. It screeched in a pitch so high my ears burned, mocking me with its dark desires. Then it happened. An emptiness so wide I couldn't breathe. It was what took over me, crushing my soul into a corner. My blood pulsed, bones crushed, the pain was almost unbearable - then it all went black.

Lola Burnard (13)
De Stafford School, Caterham

Reap

The cold wind chilled the bones of the boy, walking along the pathway. An eerie presence watched the boy from above, judging his every action. This presence was not one of a joyous nature but a morbid one. The boy felt the presence, knew of its existence and knew of its task to reap his soul. It slowly drifted down in front of him. Its glowing eyes staring him down. He knew it was his time. Darkness, all consuming visions of pure hatred swirling around the boy, filling his very soul with thoughts of pure evil. The boy's life, gone.

Harry West (14)
De Stafford School, Caterham

LABYRINTH

I stumble along, every step amplified by the claustrophobic walls around me. The beast that lays within the maze hasn't shown himself for three days. I think back to the day my family were brought here. I suppose it's the council's way of feeding the monster, it's been working for centuries. I listen for any signs of the brute that's tracking me down, suddenly a hand outstretches over my shoulder, it is pale and cracked. A searing pain travels through me, the ground rushed up towards me. I drift away from the land of the living. I am no more.

ODIN JEFFREY-DYER (12)
De Stafford School, Caterham

HER LIFE'S END

I sat in the old bathroom. The water dripping from the rusty drain, with me curled up by the window. Outside was pitch-black, a thick fog creeping over the moor. Two red eyes were peering through, looking for me. He hurt my sister and now he wanted me. All I heard was a spine-chilling scream then silence. I could hear footsteps coming up the creaking stairs. A cold hand touched my shoulder, I jumped out the window in fear of my life. Then within seconds the wicked game had come to an end.

EVIE FORD (11)
De Stafford School, Caterham

Untitled

I walked into the creepy house, chills going down my spine not knowing what's going to happen. The floorboards were creaking. My heart was racing like a formula one car. I could see silhouettes moving around. At the end of a dark passage the eyes of the creature stared into my soul. I started to approach, getting closer and closer. My heart rate got faster and faster until it pounced on me, ripping my limbs off, part by part. I started to drown in a pool of my own blood. My eyes shut and that was the end.

Ed Fisher (13)
De Stafford School, Caterham

Nathan's Essence

The sobbing gently seeped in from under the door; ever since Nathan died, the crying emitted from his spirit, never stopped. He was stuck in the infinite, torturous world of Limbo. Dad and I still didn't know how he'd died but judging from his haunting last croaks; it seemed that chilling shadows of figures in the flat were not figments of our imaginations. The last words that, to this day, still echo throughout the abyss of my mind, were: 'Sis, he's coming for you, he strolls through the hallway at dusk. I never thought his kind existed. Please - run, please...'

Jamie Lee Carter (12)
De Stafford School, Caterham

THE DOLL

The doll's eyes shifted until they were resting on Grace's eyes. The doll shrieked, 'Get away from my family!' Grace cried and threw the doll at the wall and screamed. Her parents ran for her but were puzzled at what was making her scream. That night the doll in her wardrobe pounded out like a blood-thirsty vampire attacking Grace. The next morning Grace felt terrified and jumped at any sudden noise.
Years later the mystery happened again. Child after child started disappearing hourly. Then adult after adult, dog after dog, cat after cat...

JARED READ (11)
De Stafford School, Caterham

THE CREATURE

She was sprinting down the hall, she could feel its breath tingling her back. When she reached the stairs she began to bound down them but tripped and fell. She landed at the bottom and lay there motionless. Her eyes snapped open. Her heart was pounding in her chest and she was drenched in sweat. It was all a dream she realised. A low moan emitted from somewhere nearby accompanied by the sound of footsteps getting closer by the second. She jumped up and began running but the creature was catching Chloe. She already knew it was too late...

THOMAS COOMBES (12)
De Stafford School, Caterham

Happy Halloween

It was a cold, gloomy Halloween night. I was with my mum. I would often run ahead to try and get as much candy as my miniature hands could fill. There was this one huge house which didn't normally give out sweets, however I always checked, just in case. This time it was smothered in pumpkins and skeletons, which looked so realistic.
I knocked on the door, it creaked open. There was no one, but a bowl of candy lay in the middle of the hallway. Suddenly, the door slammed shut! 'Trick or treat?' whispered the voice inside...

Jonathon Axford (12)
De Stafford School, Caterham

Missing

Dave went missing a year ago, he hasn't been seen since. No one knew what happened. It was a prank, we didn't mean for it to turn out like that. We were all friends but he took it the wrong way, it was meant to be different. We went upstairs for dinner. We started talking about stuff we couldn't tell anyone else, until three 'friends' came out with their phones recording. He ran off. I broke into a sprint chasing him. Someone started following him, he came to a cliff, he started to walk backwards and fell...

Callum Michael Strange (12)
De Stafford School, Caterham

INSANITY...

I couldn't move my hand. It wrapped around the handle of the gun, gripped so tight, my knuckles flared white. The blood was everywhere, splattered across the walls, to the ceiling, dripping from the over-filled tub. The woman inside was limp, arm hanging lifelessly over the side. *Drip*. There was a hole in her head, parts of her brain floating in the crimson tide. I glanced to the mirror, sprayed red. The smile on my face was what had changed me the most; dared me to move on. We had walked in together separate and walked out as one.

TIA THATCHER (13)
De Stafford School, Caterham

CURTAIN OF TIME

Dust blanketed the steps, rising as her footfall blew it aside. It tickled in her throat when she inhaled the small particles. Climbing the broken stairwell, a dense cobweb curled around her head, distinguishable only by the sliver of light coming through the grimy window. Then she saw it, an apparition floating above the landing. It appeared oblivious to her, as if behind a one-way curtain. Its face wore a single expression, distress. She wiped the spider silk from her eyes and watched. A second figure appeared, breaking the curtain. Their eyes locked on hers as her vision went blank.

ABBIE COOPER-BEIRNE (14)
De Stafford School, Caterham

The Winter's Night

The night was cold, the wind was howling: the trees were dancing. I shut all the windows. A storm was coming. I sat in the living room with the fire on; the curtains started swaying. I left them but they carried on. I got up and the windows were shut. Once again I sat down, the door creaked open, the fire blew out. Then I went to turn the light on. Nothing. The electricity had gone. I tried to re-light the fire but nothing happened. The windows flew open. I saw a strange figure. It was looking straight towards me.

Emily Carey (13)
De Stafford School, Caterham

Traveller

It was twelve years ago when I told him about my theory of parallel universes. Why was I so stupid? But then, at the time, he was my best friend. John Tuppence. I gave a presentation on my theory but they denied me, said it was stupid. Look at me now, Sir Jacob Smith, stuck in between two universes. John told me he had built a machine to help with my theory. He pushed me into it and I can't explain why, I got stuck here. There are noises you can't explain, things brushing against you when nothing's there...

Tabitha Wren (12)
De Stafford School, Caterham

The Holiday House

I was on holiday in a creepy house. I couldn't sleep. I heard scary noises and my things kept moving by themselves. 'I think the house is haunted, Mum. My stuff keeps moving by itself.'
'Don't be silly, the house isn't haunted. Go to bed. I will come up soon to kiss you goodnight, so go upstairs,' Mum said.
It's still scary to talk about... it was too late. I was dead and now I'm coming for you!

Sophie Daniels (11)
De Stafford School, Caterham

Don't Be Scared It's Only Me!

Katie was looking forward to getting home from university. 'Time to watch TV,' said Katie as she approached her house. She looked up at her bedroom window and saw a figure of a girl looking back at her. Shaking her head in disbelief, Katie opened the door hesitantly and called out, 'Anyone home?' An upstairs door slammed shut!
Taking a deep breath and grabbing a baseball bat Katie slowly walked up the stairs. As she turned the corner, a bright glow shone from underneath her door. Katie opened the door. There, in front of her, was herself as a child!

Abigail Louise Bland (12)
De Stafford School, Caterham

The Haunted House

At the haunted house there lived a little girl called Amy. She was a ghost. Amy died when her stepfather pushed her down the stairs. Amy comes out at night and likes to push people. Amy is invisible. No one can see her. Nobody really goes to the haunted house because she's so violent. I wouldn't go there if I were you! One night somebody was there by herself and Amy thought it would be funny to push her... she banged her head on the concrete wall. Amy just wanted to play!

Chantelle Diana Louise Bosier Martin (11)
De Stafford School, Caterham

The Awakening

When we'd moved in we knew something was wrong. Darren acted strange but the other kids were fine. Throughout the day we heard screams and during the night, crawling in the vents.
Next morning we could tell Darren was hiding something. A tear fell from his eyes and landed on to the cold quartz. There was silence this night until a bloodcurdling scream and a thump filled my ears. I ran to Darren's room only to find he was dead There was nothing but three scratches and blood staining his pyjamas. Then a cold, dark laugh filled the pale room...

George Palmer (11)
De Stafford School, Caterham

THE MAN

The door creaked open; no one was there. I slowly made my way through the house. Suddenly, a cackling laugh echoed through the hallways. Who was there? Sprinting to the door I pushed and pushed - it was locked. A silhouette became visible and a face came into sight. Over and over again I heard the same words. Suddenly, it became clear. His piercing eyes sunk into my brain, memorising me with darkness and evil. I had to escape that trap. But how? His breath ran down my spine. Was this the end? I closed my eyes and drifted away.

ELLIE MILLER (12)
De Stafford School, Caterham

THE CABIN

My cousin George mysteriously went missing in the woods so I went to investigate. Whilst I was looking I came across an eerie, abandoned cabin. I decided to look inside. I could feel something was wrong... all of a sudden there was cackling laughter. I was frightened so I tried to leave but the door was locked. I was trapped, there was laughter again. Looking around the cabin I saw some weird drawings on the walls which seemed to have been done in blood. I heard footsteps and a creepy voice whispered, 'You and George are mine now.'

TOBY KELSEY (11)
De Stafford School, Caterham

Castle House

I opened the door and the shriek of laughter reverberated through the gargantuan building. I scrambled up the passé stairs; I could hear the ear-splitting shrill of the lost boys. A door opened, I stumbled in and the balls on the billiards table were spiralling across the table. I approached what seemed to be a dormitory. The sight of empty beds swaying in the breeze sent shivers down my spine. The moans and whines of the boys shook the building forcing me to the ground. I staggered down to the basement, where I found a dark figure waiting for me...

Brooke Bowerman (12)
De Stafford School, Caterham

Baby Feet

My wife and I just bought our dream house. It's an old home. A very big one. It's a beautiful old town house, four bedrooms and two bathrooms. We started moving in today; so far all we have is wifi to watch films on our laptop and an air mattress to sleep on. We were watching Netflix in the dark before we went to sleep. Then we heard the footsteps of little baby feet, the door slammed shut and we heard a noise like laughter of a child. We don't have children! It whispered, 'Hide...'

James Furey (12)
De Stafford School, Caterham

THE GRAVEYARD

One day Morgan and Allanna were walking down the quiet road on their way to meet their friends to go shopping. As they passed the graveyard they heard footsteps behind them. They turned but nobody was there. They walked on when they heard footsteps again. The fog started creeping in. Once again they turned. This time there was a man, blood down his face, huge knife in his hand, his leg limping behind them. He made eye contact with Morgan. As he lifted the knife the girls ran for their lives. Petrified, they told their friends and called '999' instantly.

REBECCA FROST (11)
De Stafford School, Caterham

THE DEATH HOUSE

It all started in an unexplored, shuddersome territory of James' and Joe's town. No one dared to step foot on the ghoulish land but on one misty evening, they decided to explore. Without looking back, they stepped into the abandoned eerie wastelands known as 'the Death House'. The feeling in the house was unpleasing and Joe wanted to leave immediately. He staggered to the corner to get a better perspective of the horror. With a deafening cry a gruesome figure came from the opposite corner. It scuttled over to them with a deceiving smile on its face. 'Goodnight.'

GEORGE CHAPPELL (12)
De Stafford School, Caterham

Gone Girl

She sat in the church aisle, alone and melancholy. Maya's sister had been taken by *it* not so long ago. She heard the creaking of the door and she turned sharply - nothing. She faced front. She remembered the screams ejected from the house, the note her sister left telling her to go, to run. Maya's neck felt cold breath and fingers ran briskly along her arm. She froze, unable to move or speak. Heavy footsteps ran across the floor. She finally stood up and turned. 'Hello,' *it* said as she fell, unwillingly, to the marble floor.

Morgan Joyce (12)
De Stafford School, Caterham

The Silhouette

Jessica and her family moved home... to a house that was rumoured to be haunted! Her parents did not believe this myth and as they started to unpack their belongings, they gradually began to feel at home. Jessica decided to explore. Alone! Jessica walked down the creaky stairs into the basement. *Thud*, she jumped. *Thud,* it went again, and a sharp chill travelled down her spine. Jessica turned on the lights but no one was there. Suddenly, a shadowy silhouette hovered behind her. The door locked and a voice of a young girl whispered, 'Run!'

Zoe Cork (11)
De Stafford School, Caterham

Cellar Nightmare

Clara came round to find herself in a dark, dingy cellar. She didn't know how she'd got there, as she couldn't remember anything from the previous night. She closed her eyes and then, when she opened them again, she saw a dark figure coming closer. Then it was gone. Or was it? Clara was unaware as the strange figure lurked behind her with a blunt axe. He hacked the axe into her arm repeatedly, until her ruby-red blood spurted out across the room, adding to the already bloodstained walls. Clara screamed in agony until she dropped to the floor; unconscious.

Toby Cousins (11)
De Stafford School, Caterham

The Fright Of The Judges

I was sitting watching the X Factor. It was the sing-off between Anton and Monica. I was feeling sleepy just as the commentator said, 'Could it be the last we see of...'
Just then I looked up at the TV and all of the judges had turned into zombies. They walked towards me and said, 'Could it be the last we see of .....you!'
I woke up with a fright! I looked at the TV just as the commentator was saying. 'Could it be the last we see of Anton?'

It had all been a dream!

Syd Eli Darlo Fleet (11)
De Stafford School, Caterham

Brother

The boy said to the girl, 'Let's play a game. You can be the princess and I will be the monster. I will chase you!' The parents were chatting in the kitchen. The girl's mum was washing up before they put the kettle on. The mum's friend, Sandy, strolled over to the sink. 'Aww, she's so cute the way she plays with her brother.' The boy chased the girl into the woods. 'What are you talking about? She doesn't have a brother.' After that terrible day, the mum never saw her poor, little daughter ever again.

Jack Phoenix Welch (13)
De Stafford School, Caterham

The End

I was scared, alone, nowhere to go. I was deserted in a foreign land and it was getting dark. What should I do? Carry on or rest for the night? I couldn't see anything. I was in a strange world. I heard a voice, then more joined in; it was a rally of voices. Then there was a blinding light. I stumbled towards it, hoping, believing, I would make it out alive. The light grew bigger and I was deafened due to the noises. I found myself in a graveyard being watched by millions of eyes. Was this the end?

Matthew Hurcomb (12)
De Stafford School, Caterham

Just Stop!

I gulped. My body tensed as sweat drops rolled down my face and I could hardly breathe because the duvet was pulled over my head. I opened up the duvet just a little so I could get some air. I took one deep breath of air before pulling the covers back over my head. A few minutes passed. I felt like I would suffocate with the same air floating around small gaps between my body. Feeling brave, I took another peep out of the duvet, and there it was, still staring at the bed. It wouldn't stop staring...

Harry Evans (11)
De Stafford School, Caterham

Girl Loves Boy

It was a dark, ominous winter night; cold snow bit at open skin like vultures on a corpse. I was walking home from school, following the street lamps. I wasn't alone. I knew her from class, she'd tried to confess but I'd ignored her. She refused to muffle her breathing or footsteps. Her presence became a constant in my mind. I stopped and turned around. She had a grin and the glinting metal in her hand paralysed me with fear. Snow crunched underfoot as she edged closer and hugged me. 'Goodbye.' The knife slid between my ribs.

John Wyvill (16)
Reigate College, Reigate

Inevitable

Each step is another step into the arms of death. The watch hand strikes twelve and halts. Time itself has abandoned them. Eyes search frantically for what little light there is in the dark. The inescapable chill in the air settles now. Unblinking, the lone moon is the only spectator. You reach forward, blindly at first. Their breath is a mere cloud in the silent air. How were they to know that it would be their last? Nothing moves. *Slice*. Crimson droplets rush across fabric in lashes. You missed. The chase begins. Why run from death? It's inevitable after all...

Hannah Zoe Payne
Reigate College, Reigate

To Lose It All

I'm cutting through the woodlands to get home. I feel the cold wind seeping through my clothes, my skin erupting into goosebumps. There's a disembodied howl. Or maybe it's the wind whispering violently in my ears. I quicken my pace through the fallen leaves. Overhead, I hear a creak. My body freezes. I slowly look up over my shoulder. *Snap*. A dark figure tumbles out of the sky.

Helen Alvey (16)
Reigate College, Reigate

Losing Destiny

The pickup's moaning engine roared as it surpassed 56mph. *Boom!* The engine knocked out and Destiny and I were left stunned in our seats. I woke up hours later and everything around me seemed to have disappeared, as if someone had dropped a smoke bomb inside me, blocking me from the outside. I felt helpless as shocks of panic electrocuted my whole body. My heart almost jumped out of my throat when I heard Destiny scream. I reached for my phone and held my arms up high. Alas, my hopes were shattered as I read the distressing sign, 'Low Battery'.

Sharna Patten-Walker (17)
Reigate College, Reigate

The Echo Of Darkness!

Walking through this unknown place, every step I take echoes through the darkness. I feel like I'm blinded, like the undead have cursed me. I feel like someone is watching me as my nerves start to tingle. *Whoosh*. A blast of wind gushes past me and knocks me over. All I can hear now is dripping water as a puddle forms in front of me. I look around this damp, dark place, almost certain that someone, something is there. I get up and carry on moving. I freeze. Something cold is touching my shoulder!. What is it? I don't know.

Hannah Olivia Fitch (12)
Reigate School, Reigate

The Dark Cemetery

In the depths of the deep, dark cemetery the moonlight was the only light in the sky. The wind rustling the trees sounded like someone screaming in the distance, yelling for help. But why were they screaming, why were they yelling for my help? The moon stared down at me as if he knew what I'd done wrong. Misty air surrounded me slowly and the air itself became thicker. *Boom! Crash! Bang!* What was that? I looked behind me; there was a distorted shadow in the distance. *What is that shadow and what is it doing here with me?*

Sapphire Breach
Reigate School, Reigate

The Pitch-Black Graveyard

My heart wept in the pitch-black graveyard. Cracked stone steps led down to a disturbing forest. The bushes whistled in the sharp winds, voices swirled around my head, punching away happy thoughts.
A black figure stood, staring in a deep trance. My heart raced, wondering what the figure would do next? Shivers ran down my spine as the faceless figure disappeared into the treacherous night.
My sight went blurry as I tried to stay on my feet. I collapsed, lying there in desperation, trying to pull my thoughts back from the lifeless air.
Is this a nightmare I can't wake up from?

Daisy Mills (12)
Reigate School, Reigate

THE DEMON

Every step I take, I dread entering this eerie darkness. Cobbled stairs crumble down to ancient gravestones, tilting like the dead. A foul smell is followed by breath on my neck. *It's just my imagination*, I think. Drawn towards a shadow, my legs become heavier at each step, my body resists the urge to continue. A shadow determined to stay unnoticed, escapes from my sight. Suddenly, I see it. The demonic figure hypnotises me. Blood pours out of all my limbs as it suffocates me until I can't feel a thing. Then the demon possesses my lifeless, limp, dead body.

ABBIE JAYNE BUTLER (13)
Reigate School, Reigate

THE GHOSTLY GRAVEYARD

It was a dark, gloomy night and the moon was shimmering in the cold, dark sky. Jodie was walking along the graveyard to visit her nan's grave. As she was putting the flowers down suddenly the ground started to tremble. She dropped the flowers and looked around. The temple was open. *Bang.* The big oak doors of the church slammed. Walking slowly across the wet, long grass that was wrapped around her bare legs Jodie decided to go and see what was in the church. She pushed the door open. It creaked when it opened and suddenly, that was it...

NIAMH EATENTON (12)
Reigate School, Reigate

The Brick Saver

The sunlit moon hovered like an omen. We stood there, clueless. The wind whistled through the trees and the swampy grass wrapped around my legs. As the wind howled, I witnessed something I will never forget: out of the corner of my eye I saw a man with a gun pointed at me. I jerked to the left and ran. He followed me. I found a loose brick on the ground and launched it at him. I had some time. I picked up another. He shot. The bullet hit the brick and rebounded back at him. He was dead.

James Ainsworth (12)
Reigate School, Reigate

The Creature

Deep and dark, I walk into a ghost-filled graveyard. The moon glows brightly like a glaring eye. In the distance a mysterious creature haunts the set of death. The wind whistles, the spiky swamp grabs my feet. The mysterious creature starts running towards me; the air is misty so I can only see a disturbing outline. The grass is wet and slippery. I start to run. All I can hear is the thudding of the creature's feet. I slip over and hit my head on a sharp, grey rock. Suddenly I can't see anymore. Am I dead?

Kayley Tulk (12)
Reigate School, Reigate

DARKNESS

It was a dark night and the air was furiously blowing. I found an old, abandoned hospital. There were vines and weeds growing across the ground. I walked jaggedly, slowly, staring at the pitch-black hospital. I walked to the door. The door latch was rusty and torn but still unlocked. I went inside and the halls seemed like they went on forever. I stepped inside then suddenly the door shut. I tried to open it but it was locked. I looked for a way out but I saw a fleshy figure on the wall. It said, 'Quick, run away.'

JOHN RETUYA (12)
Reigate School, Reigate

THE SOUL

The moon shone upon the old, dented graves as the mysterious creature lurked in a dark and misty corner. The disturbing smell of rotten flesh was taken away by the cold, fresh wind. Grass chattered like teeth grinding together as the trees whistled and waved in the flow of the wind. I felt a shiver enter my body as the bright moon looked down at me, smiling. In the glimpse of an eye I saw a black shadow standing there, looking at me as if I'd done something, bringing bad luck to me like a black pie. It came closer.

YANDIE HANTON (12)
Reigate School, Reigate

Tendrils

I walked impatiently among the crumbling graves. *It's only a dare*, I thought, *but a scary one!* I carried on moving over the uneven gravel pathway. Thick fog hung over the tilting tombs, like the bodies had tried to push out from their doomed resting places. I reached the cold stone staircase, when my phone buzzed. My brother's name lit up the screen. 'Ryan?' I asked but a feeling of dread festered in my stomach as he gasped one word... 'Run!' Everything happened in slow-motion after that. My phone fell with a clatter as black tendrils engulfed me.

Holly Simmons (12)
Reigate School, Reigate

Monsters Are Coming

It started on Friday 13th, in the year 3,000! The whole world was full of monsters, all ugly and evil. And Tillie. Tillie was a sweet little girl whose family turned into monsters every night. She was scared every day, from the time she woke to the time she went to bed. The monsters lurked around her house making gurgling noises whilst Tillie hid under her bed, shaking as if she were outside. She hadn't any friends as everyone one was a monster. Tillie heard a bang. Her door was knocked down. That was her last moment of human dead!

Olivia Maisy Elliott (12)
Reigate School, Reigate

Running Scared

It was a cold, gloomy night. The moon was bright, the mist and fog blinding me. I was breathing heavily. I could hear sticks snapping behind me, voices surrounded me like insects.
'I'm coming for you, Jackson Wills!' a voice whispered. 'Hello? How do you know my name?'
I sprinted for the church gate. I got out my phone and called Mum. *Ring! Ring!* She picked up.
'I'm coming for you Jackson Wills,' whispered the same voice. It was next to me! I could feel its breath. Heart beating, sweating, I ran home, not wanting to return ever again.

Poppy-Rose Beesley (12)
Reigate School, Reigate

The Chop

I ran into an abandoned mansion, leaving the front door open. Inside I saw a picture of a man with rotten skin. I looked around for some loot but when I went towards the front door, it was closed. I turned around to see a man with rotten skin. He had a machete. I thought it was a dream. I tried to wake up by pinching my arm but it wasn't a dream, it was real. He was gliding towards me, ready to kill. I got onto my knees and the last thing I heard was a chop.

Sander Wijnen (13)
Reigate School, Reigate

Graveyard

I knew it was a bad idea coming to a graveyard at night. I went to look at a freshly dug grave... it had my name on it. I turned around. There was something standing behind me. I ran for the gate but it was locked so I hid in a bush. In the morning the groundskeeper came and opened the gate. I ran all the way home and crashed through the back gate and went indoors. I went up to my room. There was a note on my bed and my bed was wrecked. The note said 'No regrets'.

Kaylum May (12)
Reigate School, Reigate

The Tunnel

Shadows crept across the floor from invisible beings. Markings etched into the mold covered brickwork. Thunder-like bangs shook the cobwebs that coated the walls. Eerie footsteps followed, their sound echoing through the tunnel. As he crept forward, like a tiger stalking its prey, he sensed a dark presence behind him. He glanced back. Silence prevailed. Then it started. Howling shook the passageway and he was thrown off his feet, his brain ricocheting about inside of his head. He screamed as blades pierced his flesh and poison leaked into his bloodstream. And all he could see was the face.

Malachy Walker (12)
Richard Challoner School, New Malden

The Darkest Night Of The Year

9pm. Smith 'n' Jayson's -'Snazzy Stockings Since 1963'- Christmas party . All employees arrived at the warehouse at eight and celebrated.

11.57pm
She appeared wearing blood-red gloves which matched her blood-red lips.

11.59pm
The door flew open, the lights flickered out. Everyone froze, as if encased in diamond. 'But why now?' struggled the manager, 'why at Christmas?' The door slammed shut and 350 screams filled the night. The door opened lazily. Not a living soul was in the building.

12am
The vampire licked her blood-soaked lips as a slim smile appeared in the corner of her mouth.

Samuel Baird (13)
Richard Challoner School, New Malden

A Blind Man's Bluff

The blind man on the bottom bunk woke to a *drip, drip, drip.* He rolled over and felt a warm, thick liquid. The room was heavy with the smell of blood! He nudged his brother on the bunk above. No reply. He could hear heavy breathing. He stretched out his hand towards the dripping. He found his brother's hand, hanging over the edge of the bunk, but couldn't feel his pulse. He stretched out his hand further and met another hand in the dark. The hand held a knife.

Finn Matthew Hennessey (12)
Richard Challoner School, New Malden

The Man, The Woman And The Alley

On a dark night in an alley in the middle of Knowhere (a small town in the middle of nowhere) a woman stood, draped in shadows. She walked slowly, keeping the man in view. The man in the alley was short and, unlike the woman, was not keeping to the shadows. He ran up the alley, slamming into walls. When he got to the end of the alley, he turned, face contorted, to the woman. She approached, stopped, took in the moment, then raised her hand. On the other side of Knowhere, a scream rang out, heard by only one!

Cole Bryan (14)
Richard Challoner School, New Malden

Spine Chiller . . .

He sped through the corridor, sweat dripping from his face. Bellowing cries could be heard throughout the old mansion but he kept on going. He knew she was here, where else would that ghastly monster take her? Finally, he reached the end and grabbed ahold of the old crooked door. After immediately swinging the door open, Samuel noticed the expressionless look on the young girl's face. With all parts of her bound to the floor she revealed a bloody message: 'You're too late.'

Olivia Santoriello (13)
Rydens Enterprise School & Sixth Form College, Walton-On-Thames

Hunted

Waiting in the shadows with baited breath, he pulls a wicked looking blaster from the holster. A cruel piece of weaponry forged a thousand years ago from an ancient shard of darkness by the Sister of Sorrow. If you look close enough you can see the agonised faces of the souls the gun has claimed. There is a sharp click as Jack cocks it and the creature whirls round, snarling viciously. Panicked, he tries to force open the door. The beast ever closing in, the door finally gives way as it pounces. Jack stumbles back, poised to die, eyes closed.

Joe Mason-Coombs (14)
Rydens Enterprise School & Sixth Form College, Walton-On-Thames

Untitled

There was silence as we both stared at each other in fear. I could tell that my companion regretted announcing the story with such fearful passion. I wanted to run. The realisation was dawning on me. This wasn't just a silly story my grandad used to tell me. It was real. It was here. Suddenly, the mottled green mat was moving, writhing as if it was alive. It was coming towards us. It sucked in the light and all the hope drained from my face as I fled. Why had it left Christina's body?

Fiona Lock (14)
Rydens Enterprise School & Sixth Form College, Walton-On-Thames

Death Scythe

Susie found Death's Scythe slicing the heads off her parents. She screamed with a face full of terror, confusion, fury and sadness. Her eyes were filled with tears as Death turned around with his head tilted at a 45 degree angle to the right and a menacing grin. She was his next target and she knew that just by looking in his eyes. However, she couldn't do anything but stay frozen in place and stare. Death walked towards her and with every step he took, the more she trembled.

George Stenning (14)
Rydens Enterprise School & Sixth Form College, Walton-On-Thames

When The Forgotten Resurface

They used silver to nail the coffin shut then began an immediate scramble for the chains. Hurriedly a criss-crossing pattern was made; bright lines glimmering against black steel as the padlocks were snipped off and the ends soldered together. It wasn't until their masterpiece was stowed beneath the earth that the pastor realised he'd left his house key attached to the crucifix sealed inside the coffin and nearly swore aloud. He shouldn't have worried. Come morning both crucifix and house key were sitting on his bedside table next to a small silver nail, just slightly bent out of shape.

Antonia Bonewell Bruchhof (16)
Woking College, Woking

THERE

It's always there. You cannot see it but you can feel it. You can never lose it; once it chooses its prey there is no going back. Don't bother running, use your energy wisely. It chooses you when you are born and dies when you do. Forever suffering, you're always afraid. You'll welcome it eventually, when you accept the deadly chill that runs down your spine. The shivers will never stop but you'll stop feeling them. It's better when you do, you can put it in the back of your mind. Scary thing, the soul, isn't it? 'Yes, I am'.

ELLA BROWN (16)
Woking College, Woking

IT'S HERE

I need your help. There's this thing that's been following me the past few days. It's always there. Staring. Watching. Breathing in my ear when I turn. No one else can see it. It doesn't look human. The basic shape is there but the features are all wrong. Twisted. I've tried running. It follows me, I've seen it appear out of shadows once I thought I was safe. I'm never safe, nowhere is safe. No one believes me when I tell them, they think I'm crazy. I'm not. I swear I'm not, you have to believe me. It's here. Hel-...

CAITLYN WARD (17)
Woking College, Woking

Bathroom

The light stutters to life, swimming against the bathroom tiles. In front, a boy dressed in a cotton playsuit stands, his thumb in his mouth and his eyes wide. He glances through the mirror towards me, not wanting to make eye contact, but he knows I'm here. I'm always here. 'Mummy!'
'There's nothing there, Simon. Brush your teeth!' a voice yells. He steps reluctantly towards the mirror.
'Hello, Simon,' I say.
He jerks away, shaking his head. 'No, no, you aren't here.'
'Oh, but I am.'
He reaches for the handle as my hand lands on his. 'Let's play, Simon.'

Holly Taylor (16)
Woking College, Woking

The Clown

I lie in bed. It stares and I stare back. Its head pokes round the cupboard door, red, twine hair swaying and dangling from side to side. Its sinister smile and piercing black eyes make me shiver. *I could have sworn I closed that door*. Pulling my legs under the covers in fear of the cold breeze that tickles my toes. The door gradually begins to move and squeak. I shield my eyes with the covers as I cannot take it any longer. The prolonged squeak begins to fade. I hear it drop to the floor. Then, silence...

Oliver Thomas (17)
Woking College, Woking

YOUNG WRITERS INFORMATION

We hope you have enjoyed reading this book – and that you will continue to in the coming years.

If you're a young writer who enjoys reading and creative writing, or the parent of an enthusiastic poet or story writer, do visit our website www.youngwriters.co.uk. Here you will find free competitions, workshops and games, as well as recommended reads, a poetry glossary and our blog.

If you would like to order further copies of this book, or any of our other titles, then please give us a call or visit **www.youngwriters.co.uk.**

Young Writers
Remus House
Coltsfoot Drive
Peterborough
PE2 9BF
(01733) 890066 / 898110
info@youngwriters.co.uk